Girls'
ADVENTURE
Stories

Girls'
ADVENTURE
Stories

Purnell

SBN 361 05058 5
Copyright © 1981 Purnell and Sons Limited, Paulton (Bristol) and London
Published 1981 by Purnell Books, Berkshire House,
Queen Street, Maidenhead, Berkshire
Made and printed in Germany

Contents

Introduction

This fascinating collection of adventure stories is designed to appeal to all girls with imagination and a taste for adventure. In these pages you will find excitement, mystery, intrigue and danger. The stories will whisk you from a tiny fishing village on the coast of war-torn Thailand to the bustling souks of Marrakesh and the damp dungeons of a ruined Suffolk castle.

All the stories have been specially commissioned for the collection to provide a variety of fast-moving, exciting stories, all set in exotic or mysterious locations all over the world; but each story sharing the same vital ingredient: adventure.

Escape from Thailand

by BRENDA RALPH LEWIS

There was something floating in the water. Lanakit stood on the edge of the beach at Pattaya and peered hard at it, trying to decide what it was. It was too small and too flat to be a fishing boat, and was just drifting aimlessly, rocking back and forth with the movement of the water. Lanakit shrugged.

"Only one thing to do," she told herself. "I'll have to go and take a look!" There was no special excitement in the thought. She might well get out there in her boat and find it was just a piece of wood or a dead fish. All the same, it was something to do. It seemed a pity to waste one of the few chances she had had in recent months to get down to the beach on her own. Those chances were few and far between now that the Japanese invaders had gone to war and made themselves masters in Lanakit's country, Thailand. Lanakit's father worried endlessly these days whenever she was out of the house, even if she only went for a few minutes to Naglue market at the other end of Pattaya village. He wanted Lanakit at home, where he could see her and knew she was safe. Lanakit understood how he felt and did her best to do as he wanted, but it was very frustrating and boring, and very different from the days before the war began.

Lanakit sighed. Was it only six months ago, in December 1941, when the tiny fishing village of Pattaya had last been a

Lanakit scrutinised the long sweep of sand

peaceful, pleasant place where everyone could come and go as they pleased? It seemed like years now. In those far off days, Lanakit, her friend Thalit and Thalit's brother Pirom, had been able to spend the whole day on the beach, searching for pieces of coral or seashells. Sometimes, they would take trips to the island a little way across the water where the coral was especially pretty. They used to catch and cook a fish or two to eat during the day, and sit by the big palm trees on Pattaya beach fashioning their finds into necklaces which Lanakit's cousin Sammy sold for them from his rice stall in Naglue market. In those days, they never had to bother about things like being home before dark or not talking to strangers in Pattaya. There were no strangers in Pattaya then, and nothing to be afraid of.

Not now, though. As she ran quickly along the beach to the palm tree where she had tied up her boat, Lanakit found herself scrutinising the long sweep of sand and the road that ran alongside it for signs that there were Japanese soldiers about. She was listening, too, for the tell-tale sound of their cars or the tramp of their booted feet. Watching and listening for the approach of the Japanese had become an instinct and a habit for Lanakit. It was like that for everyone in Pattaya village, and perhaps in Bangkok and all over Thailand as well.

Lanakit reached her boat and unhitched it. All was quiet along the beach. It was very early in the morning and the fishermen were all out working in the bay. The Japanese, Lanakit presumed with a surge of intense dislike, were probably still snoring in their beds, drunk from too much sake wine last night.

"Oh, how I hate them!" Lanakit found she was involuntarily grinding her teeth at the very thought of the detestable Japanese. It was only because her father had begged her not to, in case it brought the anger of these brutal invaders on their family, that Lanakit had stopped poking her tongue out at Japanese soldiers or imitating the funny, bow-legged way they walked.

These had been only small gestures, Lanakit knew, but she just had to have some way of showing how much she detested the invaders who had taken over her country. Her father's

"But why don't we fight the Japanese and drive them out?"

brother, Uncle Chulong, who lived in Bangkok, had once told Lanakit that Thailand's name — Prateth Thai — meant "Land of the Free", but on 8 December 1941, the Thai government had resisted the Japanese for exactly five hours before they surrendered. Five hours! It was ridiculous, not even enough time to fight a decent battle! After that, Thailand was supposed to be an ally of the Japanese, but in fact they had moved in as occupiers and the Land of the Free was not free any more.

Most Thais had seemed to settle down sadly to live under the new Japanese rule, though in their hearts they prayed for the day when the British or Americans, who were now at war with Japan, would come and drive the invaders away. When that would happen, no one knew. Lanakit, however, had been too impatient to wait a single day.

"But why don't we fight the Japanese and drive them out?" she had protested to her father. "Why do we have to live like this—always being careful what we do or say in case they are angry with us? Whose country is this, anyway?" Lanakit's father had regarded her with a sad smile.

"It is our country, and the Lord Buddha knows it is ours," he told her. "When we go to the temple, and pray to him, Buddha knows who we are and watches over us in this time of trouble." He put his arm round Lanakit very fondly, realising that he was an old, tired man and she, a young, fiery and impatient girl. "Life is not so simple, my daughter," Lanakit's father sighed. "Our army is not strong enough to drive the Japanese away. If they tried, then the Japanese would cause much destruction and death, and we would be much worse off than we are now!"

Lanakit loved and honoured her father very much, as a good Thai girl should, but she was too furious and frustrated not to take the argument further.

"But the Japanese take all our rice, and our fish, and throw people out of their homes and take them for themselves!" she cried. "It is all wrong! Surely there is something we can do?"

Lanakit's father made no reply, just folded her in his arms and gave her a gentle kiss. Lanakit understood what he was

11

saying with the silent, affectionate gesture. There was nothing her father felt he could do, except preserve his family and his home and wait for better times.

Lanakit did not like to think so, and respected her father far too much to say anything, but she could not help reflecting that perhaps Uncle Chulong, who lived in Krung Thep, or Bangkok as foreigners called it, was the braver of the two brothers. Uncle Chulong had formed an escape line to China for fugitives from the Japanese army. It was terribly dangerous. If the Japanese ever discovered what Uncle Chulong was doing, they would almost certainly kill him, put his family in prison, burn down his house on the banks of the klong in Bangkok and take all his possessions. Perhaps it was because the risks were so enormous that Lanakit so admired Uncle Chulong. She only wished she could do something as brave as that to resist the hated Japanese. Instead, though, she was reduced to finding titbits of interest investigating strange objects in the bay off Pattaya beach. Lanakit fumed as she pushed her small boat down the sand into the gently curling surf at the water's edge. She hated this feeling of helplessness as much as she hated the Japanese.

Lanakit jumped in and took hold of the oars. As she rowed away from the shore, she felt the hot, damp wind of the new rainy season blowing about her face and arms. It was a good thing it was so early in the morning and the sun was not too high in the sky. Soon, though, it would start climbing and then its rays would burn down like fire, and everyone would have to keep in the shade to avoid being blistered by it.

Lanakit felt better now she was on the water. It was as if she had put a barrier between herself and the Japanese, although Lanakit knew she would have to watch out for the soldier with the binoculars whose job it was to sit on the high cliff at the western end of the beach and scan the waters around him. It was a good vantage point and the soldier was able to see almost everything that went on along Pattaya beach and in the waters offshore. Perhaps he was already spying on her, Lanakit thought, with a flicker of irritation. She turned and surveyed

Perhaps he was already spying on her, Lanakit thought

the high rock. He was not there. Maybe it was too early yet.

The object in the water was drifting towards her, and now Lanakit could see it was quite large. She quickened her rowing and pulled towards it. As she approached and saw it more clearly, she gasped. Her skin seemed to be all-over prickles and her heart beat faster.

It was a man, a tall man as far as Lanakit could tell, floating in a life-jacket, his arms and legs spread out and motionless. Lanakit brought her little boat alongside him, positioning it between him and the shore. Instinctively she glanced once again at the rocky headland and scanned along the beach, trying to see if anyone was about, but she saw only her cousin Sammy making for Naglue market with his loaded water buffalo.

Lanakit sighed with relief, and turned back to look at the man in the water. He must have been there quite a long time, for his fair skin was all patchy and red from exposure to the sun and the sea winds. A European, or maybe an American, Lanakit thought. He must be with that light brown hair and thick stubble on his chin. No Asian had that much hair on his face.

An awful thought occurred to Lanakit. Maybe the poor man was dead. He certainly looked dead, for he had not moved at all and she could not see whether or not he was breathing. Trembling just a little, for she hated the feel of dead things, Lanakit put out a hand and touched the man's cheek. It was cool, but not cold. Then, she spread out her palm in front of his nose and waited. Yes, very faintly, and slowly, he was breathing: she could feel the warmth of his breath on her hand.

What should she do next? Lanakit was in a quandary. By the European look of this man, he must be an enemy of the Japanese. That meant he was a fugitive, just like the ones Uncle Chulong was helping, but Uncle Chulong was fifty kilometres away, in Bangkok.

"Well, my girl, you wanted excitement!" Lanakit told herself a little ruefully. "Now you don't know what to do with it!"

Suddenly, as she sat there pondering, Lanakit saw a flash of light in the water. She looked up quickly. It was that wretched

Japanese, the one with the binoculars on the high rock. He was back on lookout duty and the sun must have caught one of the lenses and made the flash of light she had seen. There he was, a fat, stumpy figure perched on the topmost rock.

"I wish he'd fall off!" Lanakit thought, poking her tongue out at him. From this distance, she imagined, it was safe to do so. As she sat there, though, she realised the seriousness of the situation in which she found herself. Uncle Chulong must feel like this sometimes. Like him, Lanakit was in a position to be caught red-handed with an enemy of the Japanese. If that lookout saw her, and the man in the water, she could be in trouble.

Quickly, Lanakit judged the distance between her boat and the Japanese up on the rock. He might just be far enough away and not too high up not to see the man if she could make sure her boat was hiding him. Carefully, Lanakit pulled on one oar to bring the boat round in a quarter-circle. The boat was not very long, but most of the man was concealed. Or at least, Lanakit prayed so.

Then, a thought occurred to her. She could hold her fishing net over the side and the Japanese would think she was just out trying to catch some fish. If he spotted her at all, that is.

He spotted her. It was somehow inevitable Lanakit reflected glumly. If something can go wrong in a crisis, it always will; that was what Sammy's moody brother Tonsan always said.

Lanakit made herself sit stock still, not moving as the shout from the Japanese lookout echoed into her ears across the water. She swivelled her eyes sideways to see what he was doing, and could just make him out, standing up on the rock and pointing in her direction. He seemed to be talking to someone behind him. The second Japanese appeared a moment later, another stumpy, stocky soldier, and together he and the lookout cupped their hands round their mouths and started shouting.

Lanakit felt a flicker of fear, but she made herself go on sitting there, looking for all the world was if she was doing a bit of idle fishing. The two Japanese were waving their arms about now, trying to attract her attention.

Lanakit had formed a stubborn resolve to protect this stranger

"I can't ignore them much longer," Lankakit thought desperately. "I must do something!" If those Japanese up on the cliff took it into their heads to come out in the bay and investigate, it would be the end of everything. Not only for Lanakit, but for her father and the rest of her family, and maybe for Uncle Chulong and certainly for this total stranger whom she was sheltering behind her boat. If she did not save him, then he might become a prisoner of the Japanese.

In the few minutes since she had found him, helpless and unconscious floating in the water, Lanakit had formed a stubborn resolve to protect this stranger and do all she could to help him. This was her chance, she realised, the chance she had been waiting for: to do something really positive against those detestable little men with the cruel mask-like faces who thought they could be masters in the Land of the Free.

These two would-be masters, the two Japanese on the high rock, obviously wanted Lanakit to bring her boat in. That much she realised from the way they were vigorously waving their arms and pointing towards the shore. Best pretend she did not understand. If she appeared to be stupid enough, they might get tired of her and not bother with her any more.

Lanakit made herself turn and look in the direction of the two Japanese. She put her head on one side, and one hand to her ear, as if trying to make out what they were shouting about. One of them was watching her through the binoculars. Forcing herself again, because it was the last thing on earth she wanted to do, Lanakit smiled broadly and began to wave her arms.

"Ohio gozai mas!" she shouted as loudly as she could. "Hajime mashte?" Good morning, how are you? It was the only Japanese she knew, but it might just work to put those two creatures up on the cliff off the scent. They were poking their heads forward, trying to hear what she was saying. Lanakit went on waving and smiling and thinking how much she loathed and detested the two of them. Then, to her relief, she thought she saw one of the Japanese smile. The smile became a laugh, which echoed across the water at her. The other Japanese was grinning broadly now. Perhaps it was Lanakit's Thai accent that had amused them, but whatever it was, those few words of halting Japanese had convinced them she was harmless.

They were shouting at her again, but smiling and giving a friendly wave this time. "Sawadee! Sawadee!" they yelled. "Hello! Hello!" It was probably the only word in the Thai language they knew.

At long last, all the shouting and greeting stopped and the lookout went back to scanning the far side of the bay, in the opposite direction to where Lanakit was, while his companion stomped off presumably to go back to his own duties. A few seconds later, however, Lanakit heard the sound of a car engine.

"He's coming down to the village!" Lanakit thought with alarm. There was nowhere else for the Japanese to drive and there was nothing Lanakit could do but sit tight.

The sound of the car engine spluttering and coughing and the gears scraping as the Japanese bounced down the cliff road could be heard quite clearly in the calm morning air. Lanakit gripped hard on the rod in her hand and pretended to go on fishing. She darted a quick glance or two at the lookout who was still up on the cliff. Thank goodness he was looking in the opposite direction. Maybe, with luck, he would forget all about Lanakit and her boat.

Suddenly, the Japanese car seemed to burst into view, bowling along the road that ran beside the shore.

"Don't stop ... please don't stop!" Lanakit murmured, fixing her eyes on the Japanese in the driving seat.

He did stop. He drew into the side of the road, startling a boy and girl who were walking along by the palm trees at the kerbside. They had to jump out of the way so fast as the Japanese skidded to a halt that the girl stumbled and fell. The boy helped her up and Lanakit saw him push her behind him as if to protect her from the anger of the Japanese in the car. Getting in the way of the Japanese bullies was a crime these days, Lanakit reflected bitterly.

Then, to her alarm, she recognised the boy. It was Pirom. The girl must be his sister Thalit. Pirom was wearing his favourite longgyi again, the one with the broad red, white and blue stripes, the colours of the Thai national flag. Wearing the long-skirted wrap-around longgyi was almost an act of defiance in itself, because it was a sort of national dress for the Thais: wearing the national colours of the country was double defiance, and Lanakit knew that Pirom did it deliberately, as his own silent but deeply felt protest against the Japanese invaders.

"Oh, no!" Lanakit breathed. "Not Pirom and Thalit!" It was bad enough that she might get into trouble with the Japanese. She did not want her two best friends to be involved, too.

To Lanakit's enormous relief, there was no trouble. The Japanese in the car took no notice of Pirom and Thalit at all. Instead, he turned in the driving seat, waved in Lanakit's direction and then cupped his hands to his mouth. "Ohio gozai mas!" he yelled, in a very accurate imitation of Lanakit's bad Japanese accent. Lanakit waved back, and this time smiled with genuine amusement. "You stupid Japanese fool," she thought. "If only you knew!"

Till now, Lanakit had not dared to think of looking over the side of her boat at the man floating in the water. The Japanese might have become suspicious if she had. Lanakit forced herself to wait until the Japanese, smiling broadly and laughing to himself, drove off down the road towards Naglue market. Only when the car had disappeared did Lanakit risk a glance over the side. The man in the water had not moved. He was still floating there, unconscious, though Lanakit fancied she saw his eyelids fluttering.

She had to get him to the shore as quickly as possible. The lookout at the top of the cliff was bound to turn back towards her sooner or later. In any case, suppose the man recovered consciousness to find a total stranger staring him in the face? He might give a shout, and then the game would be up.

Pirom and Thalit were now down by the water's edge. They had recognised Lanakit and were waving to attract her attention. Lanakit saw Pirom hunch up his shoulders and bend his

"Don't ask any questions now, Pirom! Look behind the boat."

arms outwards as if to say, "What's going on?" Lanakit signalled to them to come swimming out as quickly as they could. There must have been something very urgent in the gesture which communicated itself across the distance between them, because Pirom started hitching up his longgyi straight away and began wading into the water, with Thalit following close behind. They were good swimmers, and it took them only a couple of minutes to come alongside Lanakit's boat.

"What are you doing out here?" Pirom asked, flicking the wet hair out of his eyes. "And why was that Japanese so friendly?"

Lanakit leaned forward, making a great business of laying her fishing net down in the bottom of the boat. "Don't ask any questions now, Pirom! Look behind the boat!" she whispered to him. Thalit came paddling up at that moment, and gasped when she saw the man floating in the water.

"Who is he? What's he doing here?" she trod water and put out a tentative hand to touch the man's arm. "Is he dead, do you think?" Thalit went on, her eyes widening with dismay.

"No, but we must get him out of the water soon!" Lanakit said.

Pirom had been looking the man over, and suddenly said, "He's an American—an airman!"

"How do you know?" Lanakit exclaimed.

"This is an American life-jacket," Pirom pronounced. He was very interested in uniforms and weapons and was always poring over war books and magazines. "I think he must have baled out somewhere over the Gulf. I expect his plane was shot down. There were some dogfights going on round Samut Songkhram yesterday afternoon. Maybe he was there!"

"We can't risk trying to get him into the boat," Lanakit told Pirom and Thalit. "He's too heavy for us, and the Japanese might see, but we could tow him. Suppose you two support him in the water while I row the boat—can it be done, do you think?"

"Is there any alternative?" asked Pirom.

"No."

"Then it can be done!" Pirom said firmly. "Come on, Thalit, you take his legs. Keep an eye open for the lookout."

It was an exhausting task. Between them, they attached the American's life-jacket to the side of the boat with some spare fishing line. With Pirom and Thalit holding him and swimming as hard as they could, Lanakit managed to steer the boat towards a spot at the end of the beach where a rock jutted out to the water's edge, making a narrow hideaway on the sand. Thalit scrambled out of the water and kept watch for any approaching Japanese while Lanakit and Pirom lugged and heaved and pulled until finally they managed to drag the American out of the water on to the sand. With all the rough handling he was receiving, it was no surprise that he was now beginning to stir. He mumbled a few words which Lanakit, who knew some English, could not understand.

Lanakit did not intend to stay and indulge in conversation. "Cover him up with palm leaves!" she whispered to Pirom. "You and Thalit stay here. I'm going to find Sammy. He'll help us."

Lanakit was tired and shaky after all the effort and tension of the last half an hour or so, but she ran all the way through Pattaya and into Naglue market. When she reached the stall, she found Sammy occupied in some hard bargaining with a woman over the price of a couple of bags of rice. Lanakit waited, itching and impatient at the delay. At long last, the price was agreed and the woman went off with her purchases balanced on her head.

"Hello, Lanakit. Brought me some more of your shell necklaces?" Sammy turned to her with a friendly smile. The smile faded, though, as he saw the urgent look on her face.

Lanakit looked round quickly before she spoke, to make sure no one was listening. "No necklaces!" she whispered to Sammy. "Three rice bags!" She saw Sammy's eyebrows rise a little with surprise. "Three rice bags" was Uncle Chulong's code for one foreign fugitive from the Japanese.

Speaking quickly and quietly, Lanakit told Sammy all that had happened. "You must take the rice bags to Bangkok, to Uncle Chulong," she told him urgently. "Otherwise the Japanese will get hold of them!"

Sammy looked grim. "Not if I can help it!" he said. "I wouldn't give those brutes a grain of real rice if it was up to me!"

To Sammy's chagrin, however, it wasn't up to him, as Lanakit well knew. Once a week, he had to make the six-hour journey by bullock cart to Bangkok to deliver rice to the Japanese commandant's stores there. Sammy loathed doing it, though the price the Japanese paid was a fair one, but he had no choice. This week's trip was due to take place tomorrow, and this time, Sammy reflected, it would be a lot more enjoyable. There was great appeal in the idea of duping the Japanese and helping one of their American enemies to get away through Uncle Chulong's escape line. It was the first time Sammy had had the chance to do such a thing, and he was looking forward to it. Still, it was not just a simple matter of transporting "three rice bags" to Bangkok. There were arrangements to be made.

"I'll send Tonsan ahead, this afternoon, to warn Uncle Chulong to expect the bags tomorrow," Sammy told Lanakit quietly.

"Tonsan!" Lanakit made a face. She did not take to that idea at all. Lanakit glanced across the market to where Tonsan was standing by his vegetable stall. He saw her and gave her a nod in greeting. That was something, Lanakit thought. Tonsan's in a sociable mood for once. Even so, she had never been at ease with him. Tonsan was a strange, stubborn fellow and Lanakit was not at all sure he was the right person to send on such an important errand.

Sammy was more confident. "Tonsan will do it for me—don't worry," he said. "He hates the Japanese as much as we do!"

Lanakit was not too happy about that, either. From time to time, she had the impression that Tonsan's so-called hatred for the Japanese was a bit lukewarm. Tonsan did not exactly like them, but at least, he had once said, the Japanese were Asians, like the Thais, unlike those haughty Europeans who had made themselves rulers in India, Burma, or Malaya and thought they were so much better than the "natives" of those lands.

Sammy seemed to read Lanakit's mind. "Look, he's my own brother—he's the only person I can really trust to go to Uncle

Chulong. Tonsan would never put any of us in danger."

Lanakit hoped so. She hoped so with all her heart, for if anything went wrong because of Tonsan, she would never forgive him—or herself. Try as she might, she could not help that thought running through her mind as Sammy swiftly outlined his plan to get the airman off the beach.

When he had finished, Sammy reached behind his stall and pulled out a very large sack. He surveyed it, judging its size, and decided it was suitable for the purpose he had in mind. Sammy folded it up and stuffed it into a rice bag.

"Here, take this back to the beach," he told Lanakit, handing her the bag. "Wait, though, and watch the stall for me while I go and talk to Tonsan."

Sammy gave Lanakit an encouraging squeeze on the shoulder and one of his broad, friendly grins before walking over to Tonsan's stall, where the yams, melons, coconuts and cabbages were heaped up in neat, well-arranged piles. Lanakit watched them talking. Tonsan kept nodding and Lanakit's heart sank. Tonsan was agreeing to help. Somehow, she would have preferred it had he been his usual contrary self, and refused.

When Lanakit got back to the corner of the beach where the American lay concealed, she found him sitting up, looking a bit dazed but otherwise unharmed.

"Who's this?" he mumbled, trying hard to focus his gaze on Lanakit.

"It is Lanakit—she find you..." Pirom struggled for the right words. Like all Thai children, Pirom had learned English at school, but his teacher there had never thought it would have to be used in a situation like this.

Pirom turned to Lanakit, and thankfully reverted to his own language. "I was right!" he said triumphantly. "He is an American—an American Navy pilot in fact. Lieutenant Frank Birch!"

The Lieutenant, hearing his own name among the other, to him, incomprehensible words, nodded and smiled at Lanakit. He held out his hand. Solemnly, Lanakit shook it.

"Seems I have a lot to thank you for, little lady!" Frank Birch

"Who's this?" he mumbled, trying to focus his gaze on Lanakit

murmured, managing a smile. He still felt too muzzy and dazed to grapple with the full implications of his present plight. However, one thing Frank Birch did know. When the Japanese Zero fighter, spitting gunfire into his plane over Samut Songkhram, had forced him to bale out and take his chance in the sea below, he never expected to wake up on a beach in Thailand being rescued by these three slightly-built, earnest looking children.

The American thought of his own children back home in the United States. Their main preoccupation these days was qualifying for the baseball team and getting good grades in their exams, not risking their freedom and even their lives to outwit the Japanese. Lieutenant Birch gave a deep sigh. "Jeez..." he breathed. "This damned war. This damned war." Lanakit heard him and look concerned.

"You feel bad? You need doctor?" she asked in a whisper.

"No, no... I feel fine! Fine!" Birch smiled at her. It was a lie. He felt terrible, but he wasn't going to admit that to these plucky youngsters. If they managed to get him off this beach unseen by the Japanese, it would be a miracle. Still, for their sake, Frank Birch felt he had to make the effort to co-operate in whatever they were planning to accomplish it.

Though Lanakit's English was better than Pirom's it was still not quite good enough for her to explain what the plan was. The American will find out soon enough, she thought. It was almost time for Sammy to arrive.

"Watch out for Sammy," she told Thalit. "He'll be driving Tonsan's big vegetable cart." Thalit positioned herself near the top of the rock and watched the road.

Lanakit shook out the large sack Sammy had given her and opened the top of it. "You get in sack, please!" she told Birch.

"Whaaat!" The American's blue eyes were round with surprise. What wild scheme was this? Pirom was surprised, too. His eyebrows were raised.

Lanakit felt a certain impatience. "You want get away—escape from Japanese?" she asked.

"Of course!" Birch exclaimed enthusiastically.

"Then get in sack, please!" Lanakit's chin had set in a firm line and there was a determined glint in her eye.

Frank Birch sighed, shrugged and gave in. After all, this was no crazier than what had already occurred. In any case, there was no choice. He could not hide for ever in this corner of the beach and if he tried to slip away by himself, he was bound to be seen and recognised. Even if Frank Birch could conceal his white skin and light brown hair among all the sallow, black-haired Thais and Japanese in Pattaya, his height of nearly two metres, would inevitably give him away.

"Okay, little lady!" the American told Lanakit. "I just hope you know what you're doing!"

Frank Birch was still stiff and sore from his long hours in the water but, helped by Pirom and Lanakit, he managed to crawl into the sack and wriggle it up over his shoulders till only his head was exposed. Lanakit and Pirom covered him up with big, broad palm leaves. After getting this far, it would be terrible if someone saw him and gave him away to the Japanese.

Lanakit joined Thalit at her vantage point, and they watched the road together. Sammy should be along any moment now. Sure enough, within a few seconds, a faraway rumble reached their ears. Then, the bullock cart came in sight. It was piled high with large, lumpy sacks and on top, holding the bullock's reins, sat Sammy. Next to him was Tonsan. Lanakit watched carefully. Sammy started to pull on the reins and the bullock began veering to the side of the road. Lanakit turned to Frank.

"Head down now, please," she whispered urgently. The American ducked down inside the sack and Pirom pulled up the top and knotted it together. Lanakit knelt beside the sack.

"You can breathe?" she asked.

"Just about," came the muffled voice.

"Good! Now please, do not make a noise, or shout or say anything, no matter what happens!"

Frank Birch gave a nervous laugh. "You won't get a peep out of me, little lady!" he assured her, and said a silent prayer.

Sammy and Tonsan were so close now that Lanakit could see

Sammy seemed to be having trouble controlling the bullock

the strained expressions on their faces. Sammy seemed to be having trouble controlling the bullock which was not surprising since he was pulling unevenly on the reins and giving them a small jerk now and then to unsettle the poor lumbering animal. Then, the inevitable occurred—just as Sammy had planned. The confused bullock was wrong-footed, stumbled and almost fell. In its efforts to stay upright, it crashed its weight against the shafts that held it to the cart. The cart jerked sideways, the outside wheel left the ground, the cart balanced for a second or two on its inside wheel, then crashed over on to the path by the palm trees. As it did so, Sammy gave one of the sacks a furtive push with his hand and half a dozen of them slid off, taking Tonsan with them. One of the sacks rolled towards the rock, and Thalit felt a jolt as it came to rest against it. Three or four others, which Sammy had left untied, burst open and their contents spilled out, sending coconuts and cabbages and yams bouncing along the path and down the beach.

A crowd began to gather at once. They watched with great interest as Tonsan leapt to his feet and started waving his fists at Sammy, who had somehow managed to remain on the cart. "You fool! You idiot!" Tonsan screamed at him. "Look what you've done! Can't you even drive a bullock cart?" Tonsan looked about him, at the mess of sacks and spilled vegetables. "Look at this! All my produce ruined—all because of you."

Lanakit crouched next to Thalit, watching and listening from behind the rock. She smiled. She might not like Tonsan much, but he was playing his part well. Sammy, looking ferocious with pretended rage, began scrambling down towards Tonsan.

"My fault?" he snarled. "You incompetent fool, it's your fault. I told you not to load the cart with the coconuts underneath."

Sammy pushed his face towards Tonsan's, and the two of them stood eye to eye in furious confrontation. "Spill another sack or two if you can," Sammy hissed at Tonsan. "We need as much time as possible."

Tonsan glanced past Sammy's ear and saw two Japanese soldiers on the opposite side of the road. A couple of coconuts had rolled over there, and one of the soldiers was stooping to pick them up. It occurred to Tonsan that the Japanese might be one of the honest type. He might come over and give the coconuts back and help clear up the mess. That would never do. Tonsan let himself be stared down by Sammy. He stepped back a pace or two and looked resentful.

"It's no use arguing with you," he muttered. "Let's get it all back on the cart or this lot—" Tonsan waved his hand towards the crowd that was hemming them in, enjoying the spectacle— "this lot will have free vegetables tonight!" Tonsan finished.

Tonsan's words were like an invitation. A dozen or so men and women surged forward out of the crowd and started picking up the spilled vegetables and stuffing them back into the sacks. A coconut or two and some of the smaller yams disappeared up their sleeves or beneath their longgyes, but Tonsan took no notice. Neither did Sammy. He waited a few moments, until the crowd was massed round the spilled vegetables and three or four of the men were helping Tonsan to put the cart back on its wheels. Three or four more crowded round the bullock, to keep it calm and quiet while the operation was going on.

In the middle of all the confusion, Sammy bent down, out of sight of the two Japanese soldiers on the other side of the road, and scrambled across towards the rock. "Lanakit!" he hissed. "Quickly now ... we've got about thirty seconds!" With a swift glance behind him, to make sure he was unseen, Sammy moved quickly down the beach to the water's edge, round the end of the rock and grabbed one end of the big sack which Lanakit and Pirom had started to lug towards him. Together, they pulled it up the sand to the path then rolled it against half a dozen others stacked by the roadside.

The cart was now back upright again, and one of the men who had crowded round the bullock pronounced the animal unharmed. Tonsan had managed to retrieve most of the spilled vegetables, and with the help of Sammy, Pirom and one or two of the men from the crowd, the sacks were done up, then piled back on to the cart. Lanakit stood with her foot on the sack containing the bruised, jolted and startled Frank Birch to make sure that it was the last one to be put on. At last, Birch felt himself being lifted up, then dumped down on a hard, lumpy surface. When it was all complete, Tonsan glowered at Sammy. "This time, I'll drive!" he snapped.

Sammy shrugged. "As you please ... but next time load the cart properly!" Tonsan frowned furiously, but said nothing. He turned on his heel, climbed up on to the cart and took the reins. Sammy clambered up after him, and then stretched out a hand to pull Lanakit up beside him.

As soon as the cart had rumbled a few hundred metres, Sammy gently opened the top of Frank Birch's sack. As he did so, he saw two blue eyes staring up at him out of its depths. "Jeez!" Frank Birch muttered. "What on earth happened?"

Lanakit leaned back, without looking at the American, as if she was relaxing on top of the vegetable sacks. "You escape from Japanese," she whispered out of the corner of her mouth. "That's what happened!"

Lanakit could feel the rush, crush and bustle of Bangkok long before its tall modern buildings and the ornate green and orange tiled roofs of its temples came into view on the horizon. There was an excitement about the city, a vigour that seemed to reach out into the broad flat plain of the rice fields surrounding it. Lanakit loved it, and despite the danger of the enterprise on which she and Sammy were now embarked, she was enjoying every minute of the journey to Bangkok and the prospect of seeing the city once again.

She glanced up at Sammy, sitting beside her on top of the piled up rice sacks, loosely holding the reins in his hands. The bullock had taken the road to Bangkok so often that it practically knew its own way there, and Sammy was dozing. Partly it was from the heat of the morning, partly from the green monotony of the flat countryside through which they passed and partly from the exertions of yesterday afternoon in Pattaya.

Considering Lieutenant Frank Birch was the subject of all this anxiety and activity, he seemed to having the easiest time of it at this moment. Lanakit glanced over her shoulder at the space in the pile of rice sacks which they had cleared to enable him to breathe. Down there, unseen, the American was doubtless fast asleep tucked up among the rice bags. He could afford to do so. Sammy could not enjoy such luxuries, and Lanakit gave him a gentle nudge to rouse him. Sammy started up, looked round dazed for a moment, then yawned and smiled.

"An easy journey," he commented sleepily. "No Japanese... no one stopping us..."

"Too easy, maybe," Lanakit commented. "We'd better be on the alert, Sammy. Look, there's the city!"

She could see the glittering tile roofs and flashing spires of Wat Pho, Wat Suthat and the other magnificent Buddhist temples and, shimmering in the distance, the sunlit waters of the klongs. There, she thought, Uncle Chulong was getting ready to hide the American fugitive before smuggling him further along the canal and out of Bangkok after nightfall. She and Sammy were on the last lap of the adventure, Lanakit thought with a mixture of excitement and regret. The excitement was uppermost in her mind, but Lanakit did feel a bit guilty about having to deceive her father. She had not told him why she wanted to go with Sammy to Bangkok. He had presumed that the change of scene would do the girl good, and perhaps help her to endure the boredom of being cooped up at home in Pattaya for most of the time. His kindliness made Lanakit feel worse than ever, and to salve her conscience, she privately promised herself to bring her father one of the beautiful bamboo flutes which Uncle Chulong's wife, Aunt Shabiro, made for sale in Damnoen Saduak, the floating market.

All the same, Lanakit knew her father would be horrified if he knew of the enormous risks she, Pirom and Thalit had taken in Pattaya yesterday afternoon.

None of them had felt entirely safe yesterday until they were well away from the spot where Sammy had contrived the accident. To Lanakit's great relief, though, all had gone well.

Tonsan had driven the cart to Sammy's house, and Lieutenant

She and Sammy were on the last lap of the adventure

Birch was smuggled inside. Then, Tonsan set off for Bangkok, carrying a few sacks of vegetables on the cart to make it look as if he was going to sell them in one of the markets there. Before he left, Tonsan had arranged with Sammy to meet him on the road outside Bangkok to confirm that Uncle Chulong had been alerted.

As the bullock ambled along the road towards the city and the rice cart swayed gently in its wake, Lanakit began to feel distinctly jittery when she thought about the arrangement. Any moment now, they should see Tonsan's cart coming towards them in the opposite direction, but somehow, Lanakit knew it would not happen. There was no one about, except for a crowd of saffron-robed monks who bent their shaven heads in greeting as they passed and the workers in the rice-fields who looked up briefly from beneath their broad-brimmed hats. Lanakit glanced sideways at Sammy and met his worried eyes. Maybe Sammy was thinking the same thing: Tonsan was not going to turn up. Neither of them said anything.

They drove on in silence for a few more minutes, until Sammy could bear it no longer.

"I hope nothing's happened to him," Lanakit heard him say. "Or," he added with dread in his voice "Or to Uncle Chulong!"

Lanakit felt her throat go tight with fright. Eventually she managed to say, "We can't just drive around Bangkok, Sammy! The Japanese are bound to get suspicious—you know how they watch everyone there!"

She heard Sammy sigh. "We'll have to go to Uncle Chulong, even if we don't see Tonsan!" he muttered in a strained voice.

They did not see Tonsan. There was no sign of him at all. As they entered the busy streets of Bangkok, they saw several carts coming along, but Tonsan was not driving any of them.

Sammy was desperate by now. Lanakit could see that from the way he gripped the bullock's reins with fingers so tight that his nails seemed to be biting into his palms. Lanakit sat next to him, silent and full of trepidation.

They reached the road that ran beside the klong and trundled along it until they came within sight of Uncle Chulong's house. The day had begun early on the klongs, as it always did, and there were plenty of people in the water having their morning baths and washing their hair or their clothes. Uncle Chulong's house seemed strangely silent. Lanakit comforted herself with the thought that they might be inside or on the verandah.

Lanakit slipped down from the cart and ran across the grass to where the long bamboo shutter was drawn across Uncle Chulong's living room. She lifted up the corner and peered inside. There was no one there. There was no one in the small room on the other side of the house, either. Then, she heard footsteps and a voice. She whirled round in a sudden fright, only to find Uncle Chulong standing there, his old face creased in smiles.

"Lanakit, sweetheart! How lovely to see you. How unexpected!" Uncle Chulong came towards her arms outstretched, obviously delighted to find her there. "If we knew you were coming, Shabiro would have made your favourite cholburi!"

If Lanakit had not been so rigid with alarm, her mouth would have watered at the thought of the luscious pineapple and mushroom dish that was Aunt Shabiro's speciality. "You mean you did not expect us? Tonsan did not tell you we had…" Lanakit looked round furtively before going on. "We had 'three rice bags' for you?"

When he heard that, the smile faded from Uncle Chulong's face. "Tonsan? He has not been here for many months!"

Just then Aunt Shabiro appeared, bustling out to greet Lanakit with arms outstretched. Her smile, too, vanished from her kindly face when she saw Lanakit's alarmed expression.

"Have you seen Tonsan, wife?" Uncle Chulong asked her.

"No. What is the matter, Chulong?" Aunt Shabiro breathed, realising, as her husband did, that something must be wrong.

Suddenly, Lanakit heard Sammy calling her in a tight, terrified voice. "Lanakit—come here—quickly!" She turned and ran back towards the cart, and as she did so, the sound of the approaching vehicles reached her ears. Lanakit glanced up the road in the direction of Sammy's pointing, trembling finger.

"The Japanese will search everywhere," Lanakit panted urgently

"Japanese!" she breathed, glimpsing the tight-drawn faces beneath their uniform caps.

Lanakit and Sammy exchanged frantic glances. They were both thinking the same thing: Tonsan had given them away! He had betrayed his own brother and his family! If not, then what were the Japanese doing here?

There was no time to waste wondering about it. Lanakit pelted round to the back of the cart and began pulling at the rice bags. Sammy climbed down quickly to help her, and within ten or fifteen seconds, they had extricated the startled Lieutenant Birch. Lanakit grabbed his wrist.

"No asking questions... follow me—quick!" Lanakit spoke urgently, and following her frightened eyes, Frank Birch looked behind him and saw the rapidly approaching Japanese. They were only two hundred metres away, just enough time to jump from the cart and with head down hurtle across to the house. Lanakit pushed the American down towards the klong.

"Get into the water, under the house!" she cried and ran quickly back to Aunt Shabiro. There was one way, one slim chance, to save Frank Birch from the Japanese. If only it would work. "Those bamboo flutes you make, you have one not yet completed ... without holes for playing?" Lanakit asked Shabiro. Aunt Shabiro nodded. "Yes, several of them..."

"Please, Auntie, please get one ... now ... hurry!"

The roar of the Japanese vehicles was getting closer and closer as Lanakit spoke. Aunt Shabiro bustled off and returned immediately, holding one of her uncompleted flutes. Lanakit snatched it from her without a word, and hurtled down to the side of the klong, where Frank Birch was already immersed waist deep in the water. She pushed the tube of bamboo at him.

"The Japanese will search everywhere, here under the house too!" Lanakit panted urgently. "Get under the house. You can breathe through the bamboo flute!"

The American complied at once. There was no time to wonder or ask whether what Lanakit suggested was possible. The only alternative to drowning was capture by the Japanese. The lieutenant ducked down beneath the water, and Lanakit stayed just long enough to make sure that the top of the bamboo pipe was above the surface before running back to stand by Uncle Chulong as the first Japanese car came bouncing across the grass, and drew up a few metres away. A short, stumpy officer stepped out, puffed up his barrel chest and came strutting towards them. Lanakit's hand crept out and grasped Uncle Chulong's. He held it tight and reassuringly. It helped Lanakit to make the effort to stop trembling. The Japanese gazed at Uncle Chulong without expression and bowed briefly and politely.

"I am Captain Shiksa!" he said gruffly. "You are Longgsan Chulong?"

Uncle Chulong nodded, looking the Japanese straight in the eye with tremendous dignity. Lanakit was overcome with admiration for his calm. Her uncle looked as if the last few frantic minutes had never occurred.

"We have been informed that you have an unlawful person on your premises," Captain Shiksa said in an officious tone which Lanakit thought was rather forced. It was almost as if the Japanese was speaking reluctantly, as if he disliked the task he had been sent to perform.

"I regret, sir, we must search your house!" Captain Shiksa went on. Aunt Shabiro gave a small cry of distress. "Have no fear, madam," the Japanese said with a politeness that astounded Lanakit. "My men have orders to be careful. Anything broken will be paid for."

Lanakit could hardly believe her ears. She had expected the Japanese to come barging into the house and practically take it apart in their search for the "unlawful person" they were seeking. Instead, they were polite and considerate, but they were very thorough. Captain Shiksa and his men inspected every room closely, looked behind every screen, checked every cupboard, chair, bed, table and all other furniture for the slightest sign of anything suspicious. As Lanakit had foreseen, they inspected the underside of the house, and even tested the stilts on which it stood half in, half out of the klong. Sammy's cart was included, but instead of bayonetting the rice bags, as Lanakit had thought, and spilling the contents all over the grass, the Japanese soldiers felt and squeezed them very carefully.

At last, it was all over and, as he had begun, Captain Shiksa made elaborate and polite bows to Uncle Chulong before he left.

"Many apologies," the Captain murmured. "But you understand, we cannot ignore our duty, even if…" Shiksa glanced behind him to see that his men were not within earshot, and drew a little closer to Uncle Chulong. "Even if we know the information is false, given out of spite or to settle some old score!" Captain Shiksa lowered his voice to a confidential undertone. "The young man who told us you were hiding a fugitive," he said. "I did not trust him. Oh, yes, he pretended that he was acting in the interests of friendship between our two peoples, but I think he was really trying to curry favour with our commandant. Maybe he wanted a monopoly for selling his vegetables."

Lanakit saw Uncle Chulong's face stiffen with distress. The seller of vegetables could only be Tonsan. Captain Shiksa, fortunately, did not notice the change of expression. He merely bowed very formally to Uncle Chulong and Aunt Shabiro, nodded at Lanakit and Sammy, and once more expressing his regrets, stepped into his car and departed.

There was a terrible silence for several moments after the sound of the Japanese vehicles faded away. Then, Uncle Chulong gave a deep sigh. Lanakit saw there were tears in his eyes.

"Shabiro," he told his wife. "I will not have Tonsan's name spoken in this house again. He must never come here, or have anything from us. He is not one of our family any more." Aunt Shabiro nodded. She was crying quietly, and Sammy, too, was weeping with shame and distress.

Uncle Chulong turned to Lanakit, and met her inquiring gaze.

"You expected them to be brutes, didn't you, Lanakit?" said Uncle Chulong. Lanakit nodded. "Well, you see they are not all brutes, even if they are invaders. The Japanese can be men of much culture and good taste. Simply because they are our enemies, we must not think they are savages or barbarians. And

"*I'll never sell this. This one I'm going to keep for ever.*"

they dislike a traitor as much as we do!" Uncle Chulong finished, his voice breaking. "But come," he went on, forcing himself to look more cheerful. "We have 'three rice bags' to deal with ... we have much work to do!"

Lanakit strung the last of the seashells on to the necklace, and held it up in front of her.

"That is beautiful, Lanakit!" said Thalit, who was watching. "The most beautiful you have ever made."

It was, indeed, a lovely necklace, a mass of curly white shells with little bits of coloured coral and well concealed, but visible to Lanakit, the tiny decorative pin Lieutenant Birch had given her before he left Uncle Chulong's house bound for freedom.

"In America, only very special girls are given pins like these," Frank Birch told Lanakit. "And you're a very extra special girl, little lady!"

Lanakit put the necklace over her head and arranged it carefully round her neck. It was brand new, but already so many memories were tied up in it. Memories of relief at finding that Frank Birch had survived his ordeal as he was dragged out soaking wet, spluttering and covered in a tangle of reeds. Sad memories, too, of Tonsan, who must have planned his treachery all along, while he waited for the time to use it to ingratiate himself with the Japanese commandant in Bangkok. Tonsan had not returned to Pattaya and no one knew where he was. He would probably never dare to show his treacherous face there again. Sammy, utterly mortified, had not smiled since then.

There were also guilty memories. Lanakit's father, when she confessed everything to him, did not know whether to give her a hug and kiss for her courage or punish her for deceiving him.

Frank Birch's pin winked and sparkled at her out of the froth of little shells. Thalit came over and inspected it admiringly.

"You could get a good price for that in Naglue," Thalit said enthusiastically. "Sammy could sell it for many baat!"

"Oh, no!" Lanakit smiled at her. "I'll never sell this. This one, I'm going to keep for ever!"

The Garden of Peril

by SUSANNAH BRADLEY

Paula arrived at her grandmother's cottage on a beautiful sunny day at the end of July. It was a long walk up from the village, where the bus had dropped her, to the long, semi-detached cottage which stood by itself, and Paula could hardly wait for some of her gran's home-made lemonade in the cool of her stone-walled kitchen. She walked past the new estate on the edge of the village and on past the doctor's house, set back from the road, and then there was nothing but open fields until the telephone box at the crossroads, where she turned right. A little farther on was the cottage, and there was her grandmother at the door, looking out for her through the waving hollyhocks in the front garden.

Paula waved, and so did Gran, jumping around on tiptoe like an excited bird. While Paula thought how amazing it was that her grandma should be so lively at her age, she noticed the dark shape of someone moving behind her in the doorway; strange, that was, because Gran lived alone, and the other half of the cottage had been unoccupied since old Mrs Hubble had died last year. Paula could not understand why she suddenly shivered.

"Why Paula, I'd hardly recognise you!" called her grandma as Paula came up the path. "You've grown so much in a year!"

"I know! I've grown out of everything! How are you, Gran?"

Paula waved, and so did Gran

"Fit as a fiddle," was the cheerful reply. "Come on inside. A nice cool drink is what you must be wanting." They went inside, and there, at the table, stood a stout, elderly woman with grey hair and a stern expression.

"This is Mrs Parfitt," said Gran. "Mrs Parfitt, meet my eldest grandchild. Mrs Parfitt's taken the place next door. She has been here for several months now. Nice company for me, she is." Mrs Parfitt forced a smile and looked Paula up and down.

"Come a long way, have you?"

"All the way on a train and then a bus, all by herself!" said Gran. "Managed the change all right, did you, dear?"

"It was easy," said Paula. "I remembered where to get the bus from coming with Mum and Dad last year, and there wasn't long to wait." Gran poured the lemonade from the stone jug.

"And how is everyone? Little David must be quite a man now, starting school in September."

"Oh yes. He drives Mum wild, wanting to play schools with her all the time, and Nancy's had her pigtails cut off."

"Well, bless me, I can't wait to see them," said Gran. They talked for some time about Paula's family and then Paula said,

"Dad wants to know why you don't come and live with us now we've got the bigger house. There's plenty of room and you'd have your own bit of it, you know." Mrs Parfitt frowned.

"Oh, well... you know me, I'm a bit independent," laughed Gran. "Do have one of these caraway buns. Mrs Parfitt made them specially." Paula bit into one.

"They're lovely, Mrs Parfitt."

"Glad you like them," said Mrs Parfitt. "I do a lot of baking."

"Have you a big family, then?" asked Paula, politely. There was a pause.

"No. Just me. But I help your grandma out now and then."

"And very grateful I am too," said Gran, patting Mrs Parfitt's shoulder as she moved past her to the stove. "But today I've done my own baking and there's a chicken in the oven. It isn't often I get a chance to spoil my granddaughter, and it's all nearly ready now. I've only got to make the gravy, so don't you go filling yourself with cakes or you won't do it justice."

Mrs Parfitt stood up. "Well, I'll be going then, Mrs Rose, so you can get your meal. Nice to meet you, Paula. I'll see you tomorrow, I expect."

"She's a nice woman, but she does get under my feet sometimes," said Gran, as they laid the table together. "She does not have a family of her own, you see. Not even far away, and she's been a widow for some time, I believe. Her husband's family lived near here, and he always talked about living here when they retired, but they never got round to it, so she ended up coming on her own when a place became vacant."

Paula did not want to talk about Mrs Parfitt. "How's the garden, Gran?" she asked.

"Not as good as I'd have liked. Slugs! Never seen the like. We had such a wet June, you see. They ate everything in sight. Luckily they don't like tomato plants or I'd have nothing left at all. Are you still interested in plants, then?"

"Oh yes," said Paula. "Do you know what I'd like to do, Gran? When I leave school? Go to one of these college places, like Kew Gardens or somewhere, and learn all about botany so I could get a job working in gardens."

"Funny sort of occupation for a girl," said Gran, as she carved the chicken. "I would never have thought you'd go for a job like that. Why not a nice whizz-about sort of life, an air hostess or something? That's what I'd do if I had the chance."

Paula laughed, picturing her grandma as an air hostess. "I don't know. It's just how I'm made."

Paula slept well that night, under a pea-green eiderdown which she had to kick off in the early hours. The heat was obviously going to last, and she wanted to be up early to water the garden for her grandma before the sun got round to it, but the change of air, the comfortable bed, and the long journey of the day before all conspired to keep Paula sleeping on until past nine the next day. She woke to hear voices downstairs, and sat up, wondering for a moment where she was.

She came down to find Mrs Parfitt making a pot of tea, while

Mrs Parfitt looked at her with pale green eyes

Gran, on seeing Paula, broke an egg into the frying pan beside a sizzling slice of bacon. "Hello, slept well?" asked Gran. "Your breakfast's ready."

"Good morning," said Mrs Parfitt. "Not an early bird, are you? I've just popped in to see if Mrs Rose wants anything from the village. I'm just going there."

"Oh, let me run the errands!" said Paula to Gran. "It'll save Mrs Parfitt's legs, and I'd like to."

"Very well," sniffed Mrs Parfitt, putting down her half-empty teacup. "If you think my legs need saving, I'll be off."

"Oh, I didn't mean—I'll get your shopping too, if you like," said Paula hastily. Mrs Parfitt looked at her with pale green eyes which were narrowed, like those of a cat. Paula shuddered.

"No thank you," she said, quietly, and went out.

On her way out of the garden, Paula scanned the horizon to see if Mrs Parfitt was ahead of her. Perhaps if she walked down with her, she could put things right, but Mrs Parfitt was not on the road, and as Paula turned to wave to Gran she caught a glimpse of the neighbour's pink apron as she moved sharply away from an upstairs window. Odd, thought Paula. She's gone in and is spying on me. What a strange woman, and such wierd eyes, just like a cat.

The shopkeepers remembered Paula from the year before, and what with stopping to chat, and dawdling home looking for wild flowers, it was quite late when she got home. There was cold chicken and salad for lunch, followed by apple pie and custard.

"I hope I didn't upset Mrs Parfitt too much this morning," said Paula thoughtfully, as they washed up.

"Oh no. She's been in since. She brought that apple pie, and some seed buns for our tea," said Gran. "What will you do this afternoon?"

"Sunbathe, I think," said Paula.

It was very hot in Gran's garden. Paula tried to read for a while, but her eyes began to hurt and she felt a bit sick. After a while she went in to lie on her bed; but soon she felt even worse, with pains in her stomach. Gran was getting very worried.

"Perhaps you ate too much at lunchtime," she said. "You should be like me — I never eat puddings, you know. That apple pie must have been too much for you."

"It's just a touch of the sun," gasped Paula. "I'm sorry to be such a nuisance. I'll try to get some sleep now."

She dozed for a while, and when she woke, the sun had gone down and Gran was coming in with a tray of tea and two of Mrs Parfitt's seed buns on a plate.

"I've just had the same as this for a snack and I'm off to bed," said Gran. "I thought you might be feeling up to a little something." Paula smiled weakly and Gran said goodnight. Alone again, Paula felt the need of some air, and went to lean out of the window. Moonlight was illuminating the whole garden and that of Mrs Parfitt next door. The cool evening air made Paula's headache lighten at once, and for a while she leaned out, feeling refreshed at last.

Suddenly she stiffened. Mrs Parfitt was picking foxgloves at the bottom of her garden! This was a strange time of the day for flower-arranging, wasn't it? Paula glanced at her watch. A quarter to ten at night? And foxgloves, too.

What was the matter with foxgloves? Why should that thought have come into her mind? Then she remembered. They were poisonous; she had read it in a book, and made Dad dig up those in the garden at home, because of David. But most people did not know foxgloves were poisonous. They grew them because they were pretty.

Mrs Parfitt straightened up and walked to the end of her garden where a wild area ended in a bank. Paula peered through the gloom. Mrs Parfitt was stroking the fat, green leaves of a plant with rich red berries at its heart. Lords and Ladies, thought Paula, and because she had been thinking of the foxgloves her mind immediately gave her a nudge, so that she started, as if to say, "These are poisonous, too," and Lords and Ladies never grew in a cultivated garden by accident.

Mrs Parfitt came slowly back up the path, and to the watch-

Mrs Parfitt was picking foxgloves at the bottom of her garden

ing Paula it was as if she was giving a guided tour of her plants, stopping at first one, then another, to admire. And every plant was poisonous!

Surely it had to be a coincidence? As Mrs Parfitt went indoors, Paula searched her bag for the plant book she carried everywhere. It took a long time to check out each plant she recognised, but at last she had to face the truth. Leaves, flowers, seeds, perhaps only part of each plant was dangerous, but each one had something. Mrs Parfitt grew only poisonous plants!

Something clicked in Paula's mind. That apple pie... her queasiness since... There had been seed buns, too!

Paula ran to the dressing-table and switched on the lamp which stood there. She broke one of the seed buns in half, and picked out one of the seeds. They were too large for caraway or poppy, and not the same shape. More like ... delphinium seeds! Which were poisonous!

In Mrs Parfitt's garden the tall delphinium heads swayed grandly in the moonlight. Paula stared at them in horror. Gran! She had eaten some of those buns! She ran along the landing to Gran's door, and knocked.

"Gran, are you all right?"

"Whossat?" came Gran's voice, blurred with sleep. Paula went in, but Gran did not look up at her. She lay on the pillows, her head lolling to one side, mumbling. Paula tried shaking her awake, but all that happened was that a bit of white froth appeared at the corner of Gran's mouth.

Paula flew downstairs and came back with a glass of salty water. She forced the liquid into her grandmother's mouth and made her swallow it but holding her nose until she did. Gran spluttered and gasped, and was sick. It was an awful mess, but Paula was too frightened to care. She mopped up as best she could, while Gran groaned and opened her eyes.

"Poison, Gran. Mrs Parfitt's been poisoning us."

"Silly child," said Gran in a weak voice. "Why should she do..." Her voice tailed off and she was asleep again. This time Paula could not wake her. Then, from the other side of the party wall, came a harsh raucous cackle. Mrs Parfitt was laughing.

Suddenly, Paula felt a fresh upsurge of fear; there they all were, Gran, Mrs Parfitt and herself, all under one roof with only a wall to separate them.

Paula ran for her anorak and bolted down the stairs. She had to fetch help. Checking that there was money in her pocket, she flung open the front door. There in the moonlight, shuffling down the path, was Mrs Parfitt.

"Going out at this time of night, dear?" she said. Paula, gripped by fear, backed indoors again. Mrs Parfitt followed her in and closed the door behind her.

"Now come along and don't be silly," said Mrs Parfitt briskly, moving past her into the kitchen. "I'd just finished watching television and I heard such a dashing about next door, I thought I'd better see if there was anything wrong. I'll put the kettle on."

Panic ebbed away from Paula. Mrs Parfitt seemed so normal. Perhaps she was being silly. She sat down at the table and presently Mrs Parfitt put some hot coffee in front of her.

"You know," she began, shakily, "I thought..." She stopped. There was an odd gleam in Mrs Parfitt's eyes as she stared at the coffee in front of Paula, those narrow, green cat's eyes. The picture of Mrs Parfitt in her poisonous garden flashed across Paula's mind, and before she knew what she was doing she was running out, down the path and into the lane as fast as her legs could carry her.

On she ran, stumbling over the stones until she reached the phone box. Her hand was on the door and she was about to go in and ring 999 when she heard Mrs Parfitt calling her name. Remembering the doctor's house outside the village she ran on, gasping now, her stomach heaving, afraid that Mrs Parfitt would catch her before she could get help.

The doctor's light came on within seconds of her ringing the doorbell, but to Paula it seemed an age before he had opened the door and was listening to her story. Safe in his car, speeding back to the cottage, she was filled with panic for Gran, left alone at the mercy of that strange woman.

"I'm sure you're wrong," said the doctor, calmly. "She and your grandmother are the best of friends."

Gran's bedroom was in darkness. The doctor switched on the light. The bed was empty, and she was nowhere in the cottage. The doctor was showing signs of worry now. They raced next door and the doctor forced his way in.

Mrs Parfitt was leaning over Gran's still form, which lay inert on the living room floor.

"Keep away!" she snarled. "I'm nursing her! I've no one of my own but her! She's mine!" Her green cat's eyes flashed as she advanced, and Paula saw with horror that she had a knife in her hand. She flew like a tigress at the doctor, but he was too strong for her, and at last she was lying, sedated, on the sofa while the doctor examined Paula's grandmother.

"She'll be all right," he said at last to Paula. "Now run to that telephone box and ring for an ambulance."

Much, much later, with Gran and Mrs Parfitt in hospital, Paula slept in the doctor's house. At breakfast she met the doctor's son and daughter.

"Dad says you can stay here," said his daughter. "He says you'll like talking to our Mum. She's a botanist." Paula's spirits rose. Things were looking brighter, and so was her grandmother, when she visited her later that day.

"You mustn't blame that poor Mrs Parfitt," said Gran. "She was unhinged, you know. They'll be putting her in a home to look after her. Jealous of you, she was! I wonder who'll move in next door to me now?"

"Gran, you're amazing!" laughed Paula. "Something good came out of it, anyway. The doctor's wife knows all the horticultural colleges I could apply to when the time comes, and their Sarah's my age, she's ever so nice. Oh Gran, I'm sorry this happened, but..."

"Everything has its uses, eh?" smiled Gran. "Poor Mrs Parfitt. Even she did some good, even if it *was* by mistake!"

For the Love of Agosto

by ANGUS ALLAN

The round, sad eyes of the donkey shed no tears. Even though Andreas grunted with the effort and shook sweat from his face as he plied the thin wand of peeled, whippy bamboo, the grey animal stood there, unflinching; but its head hung down, and its long ears drooped towards the sun-baked troughs that ran between the vines on the hillside terraces.

"Stubborn, foolish beast." Fat Andreas threw down the stick and stood back, panting. His weather-beaten face broke into a lopsided grin, and he turned to Doulla, spreading his hands. "You see, little one? All donkeys are the same. No sense. I could light a fire under him, and he would not move."

Doulla Domassou's expression gave nothing away. Her eyes were fastened on the cowering beast, sagging beneath its burden of panniers, each almost filled with harvested grapes. "He might move if you spoke kindly to him," she said.

"Kindness? There is precious little room for kindness in this unhappy Cyprus of ours," grumbled Andreas. "Work, that is all. Hard, hard work. If we are to survive."

Doulla, twelve years old, looked at the man with eyes filled with a wisdom far beyond her years. One might have seen, in the depths of them, something of the island's immediate, turbulent past. She had lost her father and her mother in the fright-

"I know that, Uncle, and I am grateful."

ful violence that had followed the sudden Turkish invasion: the fearful period when the nights had been made hideous with the racket of sub-machine guns, the screams of those who fled the terror; when homes were destroyed, and belongings hurled from houses and set alight in village squares. And one might see the snarling faces of invading soldiers, looting and killing.

"I would never have beaten Agosto," she said.

"Agosto?" Andreas, the half-uncle who had taken Doulla in after her flight south beyond what the Turks now called the Attila Line, laughed out loud. "Dear child. Your memory is at fault. There must have been times when your precious Agosto was just as infuriating as this miserable creature here." As if to underline his words, he picked up the stick again and swished it through the air.

"He was my friend," Doulla insisted. "I loved him. Papa gave him to me when I was three years old, and we grew up together. He was a clever donkey," her voice trembled as she dropped it almost to a whisper, "and I had to leave him behind."

Andreas, who in truth had his own problems in the divided island, with the Turks in the north and his own Greek-inspired government in the south, had no time for such talk. "It is more important, Doulla," he said irritably, "that you realise how much your Aunt Elena and I have done for you. You are an orphan. We keep you, at much expense. We treat you as we treat our own sons, and things are not easy. I tend my vines and sell my crops to the buyers in Nicosia. From dawn to dusk I work in this infernal sun, just to keep us all alive."

"I know that, Uncle, and I am grateful." Doulla bowed her head. Her eyes took in her dress—a relic of former days, patched where her work among the vines had torn it, but she saw her shoes, which Uncle Andreas certainly had provided, and the heavy woollen socks, wrinkled and drooping, that her aunt had knitted for her. She knew that she did owe them her survival. Then her gaze fell again on the helpless animal Andreas had been beating, and the memory of Agosto came back, more strongly than ever. "He was small," she said, "but we taught him some tricks. You should have seen him walk over the plank that we laid over our waterhole; and with a straw blindfold over his eyes!"

Andreas, who had been checking the tightness of the pannier-straps, threw his hands into the air. "Your father was a fool to bother with such things. Donkeys are no more than beasts of burden. Look, Doulla. Was your Agosto clever enough to run away with you when the Turks came? No. He stayed behind, like the ass he was, to be eaten by the invaders."

"Even Turks do not eat donkeys," said Doulla, hotly.

Andreas spat in the dirt. "Pah. Those barbarians would eat rats. And what if Agosto escaped their cooking pots? I tell you they would beat him daily, and he'll fare much worse than this lazy, no-good animal of mine." Anger had taken hold of the man now, and he turned his back on the girl. "There are many things you have to do here. Be off to your work."

Sadly, Doulla walked away, hearing behind her the renewed hissing of the bamboo and the irritable grunts of the man who wielded it.

There had been no chance of comfort from her Aunt Elena. A stern, uncommunicative woman, she encouraged no conversation as she and Doulla milked the family goats. Nor was there much hope of sympathy from her cousins Vassiliou and Gregoris. Both in their early teens, the black-haired brothers spent most of their time mocking Doulla's mountain accent, for they were lads of the lower-lying hills, with their own friends and their own low opinion of the girl. She remembered the first day she had arrived, weary and dirty. A typical refugee. "What do we want with Doulla?" Gregoris had sneered. "Mountain people know nothing except how to scramble among rocks, like overgrown lizards. And their fingers are good only for picking cherries." It had meant a fight, of course, quickly broken up by Andreas, but nonetheless undertaken in deadly earnest. Still, sometimes, the boys would taunt her when their father was not around, and there would be silent scuffles at the back of the cottage. Even though she often beat them, they would never tire of their usual taunt. "Who ran away from the Turks? You were not so bold against them, cherry-picker."

Doulla lay in bed that night, but on top of the patchwork blanket spread across her straw-filled mattress. Her small oil lamp still burned on the shelf beside her, and round it, their wings clapping audibly together, fluttered the big scarlet and grey moths—the same kind of moths that she had always welcomed into her room back in the pine-scented village of Ayios Georghios, high in the Troodos Range, far beyond the spinal summit of Mount Olympus. The girl was fully dressed, for a determination had entered her mind that evening. A determination that simply would not leave. She got up. Around her, the house was still and silent, but outside, as she carefully pushed back the slatted shutters, the night was loud with the cry of crickets. The sweet, heavy air, full of mimosa, warm and beckoning, seemed to surround her like a protective cloak as she slipped over the sill and dropped to the ground, cushioned with layer upon layer of fallen fig leaves. Doulla looked up into the sky, and there, blazing brightly, was the Dipper. The Great Bear. The constellation that pointed north towards the pole star. She looked back, and though she heard the soft snoring of Andreas, she did not hesitate. "Forgive me," she breathed. "I know this is silly, but I want my Agosto. He's mine. We belong together."

Gods may have looked down, and scoffed. There was Cyprus, slashed apart by a line, above which Turks held rule, below which Greeks stood guard against any further penetration. Between the two there lay a corridor patrolled by troops in blue berets: Swedes and Irishmen and Danes, all members of the United Nations Peacekeeping Force, armed to keep the anatagonists separated. And upwards, ever upwards, under cover of night, a mere girl of twelve was about to venture into this dangerous area. A girl of twelve, unprotected and alone, looking for—a donkey.

Nearly three hours had gone by, and a thin sickle moon hung over the steep slopes, scattered with olive and pomegranate, littered with stones and hard-baked clods of earth. She had followed winding goat-tracks, had slaked her thirst from trickling streams. Fruit that she had plucked on her way had sustained her, along with the hunk of coarse bread she had carried in her hand. Beyond her, the pine-clad mountains were black sentinels against the indigo sky. Noiselessly, she sank to the ground as the faint sound of voices came from somewhere away to her left. Doulla could not understand the rich brogue of the two men who passed, unseeing, within a metre of her, but she knew by the green, white and orange of the badges on their shoulders that they were Irishmen, for she had seen them often enough on the road past Andreas's cottage. They would never harm her, but they would send her back, so she kept perfectly still until their chatter died away.

A road, now. Neglected. Its once firm tarmac rutted by the passage of military vehicles. A weatherbeaten tin sign that pointed to Platres and Troodos and Mavrovouni beyond.

On and on, Doulla flanked the broad slopes of Olympus and hurried through thickly gathered conifers, the fallen needles crackling disturbingly beneath her feet. Once, the harsh cry of some night bird brought her heart into her mouth. It seemed so long since she had heard such things and, in those days, she had taken them for granted.

It was nearly four o'clock in the morning, though she had no watch to tell her the time, when Doulla reached the line. She was working downhill now, and she had expected at least a barrier of barbed wire, but there was none, only a cleared strip in the lower forest, perhaps some hundred metres wide. She lay prone among stunted bushes, and waited while a land-rover, without lights, but with the azure and yellow three-crowned badge of Sweden emblazoned on its door, clattered past. Four men, blue helmeted, sat in the back, rifles held upright between their knees. So far, so good. They would be on the lookout for parties of guerrilla saboteurs, perhaps for smugglers, always ready to make a grisly profit in a divided land, but not for a solitary girl.

At a flat run, Doulla picked herself up and threw herself across the open ground. No challenge came to her ears as she stopped,

She had expected at least a barrier of barbed wire

panting, in the shelter of the far trees. If there had been anyone to see her in the gloom, he would have detected the triumphant flash of her teeth as she stood recovering her breath.

Then she went on again: on and on in increasingly familiar country. A roadside well—she knew it. The stump of another signpost—torn down, she supposed, because it had been lettered in Greek. The big, dead fig tree, grotesquely split by lightning many years before, that stood by the fork in the road above her own childhood village of Ayios Georghios. Doulla read the sign. It had been re-named Türbe by those who lived there now. She did not know that it was the Turkish word for "tomb" or that it was in honour of Turkish soldiers who had been ambushed there by partisans of her own race.

She sat down on a fallen trunk. There was still a good hour to go before dawn, but there was still light enough to pick out the village itself, just beneath her. There was her father's old house, and the ramshackle stable beside it where Agosto had been kept among the implements with which they had all tended the peaceful orchards. Doulla felt a lump rise in her throat, and blinked away the sudden tears of bitter memory.

Suddenly Doulla felt a rush of despair. She had felt no fear in her long journey through the night, for the thought of being re-united with her beloved Agosto had been uppermost in her mind, but here, at the end of her quest, the bitter voice of reason sang in her ears. What a fool she had been! As if Agosto would still be here, in his old stall, waiting for her! As if the Turks would simply have left him there! Despite herself, she began to cry, softly and silently. "I don't know where you are, Agosto. I don't even know what you look like! You, you wouldn't recognise me after all this time!" All the hopelessness of her own unhappiness welled up and flowed over. It had been madness. Sheer madness. And what would Andreas say? What would Aunt Elena do to her? Worse still, how could she bear the taunts of her cousins? Remorse and exhaustion took their toll, and slowly, she keeled over sideways until her head touched the ground, and her eyes gradually closed.

"Izminizi!" The sharp command snapped Doulla awake, no less than the boot that stirred her ribs. Eyes wide, she stared up into the glowering face of a man in olive-green fatigue uniform, a water-bag hanging limply from his right hand. In that split instant she took in the glare of the morning sun behind him, the thick moustache over his thin, tight lips, the rifle slung loosely over his back.

"Izminizi," he snarled again. "Your name."

Instinctively, Doulla drew back her right leg as if she meant to get up. Then, convulsively, she shot her foot out and caught the solidier beneath his right knee. As if in slow motion, she saw the empty water-bag curve lazily into the air as he toppled, thrown off balance by the ferocity of her move. His mouth was open. She saw cracked, stained teeth, but no sound came before all the breath was knocked out of him as his back hit the hard, unyeilding ground.

The girl was on her feet before the winded man had stopped rolling. Snap images swamped her mind as she took off up the hillside: a red flag with its white crescent and star, flapping in the morning breeze to her left; a startled bird, rising from the bushes in front of her, screeching in her face. Then, inevitably, the hoarse yell from behind, and the sinister clack of metal on metal as a rifle bolt went home!

In a dream, when one runs from danger, one seems unable to move one's feet. In real life, there is no such problem, and yet the brain, insanely, crowds one's head with triviality. Doulla could almost see her two mocking cousins, boasting of their own clashes with Turkish troops during the invasion. "The bullets," Vassiliou had bragged, "whistled past my head." Now she knew that he had been lying, for bullets do not whistle. They snap. Like whip-cracks. Shot after shot broke the air about her ears as, gasping for breath, Doulla reached the shelter of the trees. The balloon was well and truly up, and she had no doubt of the terrible fate she would suffer if they caught her. Never mind the current partition of the island, she had been brought up in centuries of hatred between Turk and Greek, and believed

"Ah, well, it looks like a Greek, doesn't it?"

them, unfairly perhaps, to be little more than savages; as they, indeed, would have regarded her.

Inevitably, like a rabbit pursued by hunters, she lost her way. Ducking hither and thither, she found that the forest of her childhood, once so friendly, had become an enemy, and all the while the shouts of pursuit, for pursuit there was, came closer.

Worn out, unable to run another metre, Doulla threw herself into the cover of a deep patch of scrub and tried to silence her gulping in the soft litter of leaves. Off to one side, she heard the trampling of the Turkish soldiers, their raucous shouts. In a moment of horror, she heard two of them turn towards her.

Then, from just ahead of her, the bushes parted, and a donkey ambled into view, cropping here and there on the sparse vegetation. Doulla stared at it, hearing the Turks break into coarse laughter. One said to the other, "Nothing there. Just one of our lop-eared friends." His friend replied, "Ah, well, it looks like a Greek, doesn't it?" They laughed again. Of this, Doulla understood not one word, but she did appreciate her luck as the two soldiers turned away to follow their rapidly receding comrades into the trees.

The donkey left off his cropping, and looked towards her. She realised that it knew she was there. Very, very slowly, Doulla sat up, her heart racing. The donkey drew close and nuzzled her. "No," she said aloud. "No. It cannot be. You are not Agosto?" Clearly, such a coincidence could not possibly have happened. Doulla shook off her tiredness and clambered on to the animal's back. "No matter," she whispered softly. "Fate has brought you to me. I cannot refuse your help."

No stubborn beast, this. Placidly, the donkey threaded a hidden path up through the rising mountains. Never once faltering, it came to a natural ravine, just below the far rise of the ground towards the de-militarised zone and the reach of Mount Olympus. Dizzy with fatigue, Doulla was at least conscious of the sure-footed animal picking its way, with practised ease, across a fallen tree that spanned the dizzy drop, and this with the high morning sun in its eyes, more blinding than any straw mask.

"You, you are Agosto!" The donkey snorted, just once, and even Andreas would have sworn that there was an expression of deep contentment in the soft brown eyes.

Far beyond the limits of Turkish domination, well across the corridor of the Attila Line, a squad of Irish troops intercepted the gently stepping animal and its sleeping burden. Sergeant Patrick Kelly, from Mullingar, said, "What have we here? A wee brat on a cuddy—and the pair of them near enough done for." Doulla opened her eyes, scarcely conscious of the friendly faces beneath the blue berets. She breathed one word, "Agosto."

"Agosto!" Sergeant Kelly turned to his patrol and grinned broadly. "Now, how do you figure she knew that? Our password for the month—the Greek for 'August', and you'd never think anybody would use it now, in October!"

"She'll be okay when we get her back to camp and put some food in her, sarge," said one of his men. "Her and the moke, both." Gentle hands lifted Doulla from the donkey's back, and equally gentle hands led the animal after her through the trees.

Two days later, Doulla rode back into the yard behind the cottage. She was escorted by the amiable Irishmen who had come to look on her as almost a kind of mascot, and to give them their due, neither Andreas nor his wife Elena showed anything but relief for the girl's safe return. Even Vassiliou and Gregoris kept their mouths shut, respectfully, when they heard of their young cousin's adventure across the forbidden zone. There would be no more talk of "cherry-pickers" from that quarter.

None of them, however, actually believed that the donkey was Agosto. Only Doulla held fast to that notion. But she felt it was significant that, out in the vineyards, Andreas never once peeled himself a bamboo again, and even treated his own animal with a new respect. It might be laden with panniers in the picking season, but instead of adding his own vast bulk to the load, Andreas would sigh, pat the grey neck, and with a cautious glance at Doulla, say, "Come along, old fellow. You and I have a market to reach." Agosto and Doulla would follow, smiling, as befitted hero and heroine.

The Marrakesh Mystery

by SUSANNAH BRADLEY

Jenny Bailey was going abroad for the first time in her life. Even now she could hardly believe it was happening, though the plane was about to touch down in the mysteriously romantic land of Morocco.

"This is a bit different from Devon," joked her father, smiling at the young Arab who had introduced himself to them almost as soon as they boarded. "We felt it was time that Jenny saw a bit of the world, so her mother has taken her younger brothers to Devon while we fly off to the sun."

"Oh, Dad, how can you talk about Devon when we're arriving in Marrakesh?" cried Jenny. "Isn't it exciting, Mahmoud? Oh, I forgot, you live here, so it must be very ordinary to you."

"You are right, it is home," he said, "and you must let me help you to feel at home, too. Please allow me to be your guide as you tour the sights."

"Oh, that would be very kind," said Mr Bailey, doubtfully, "but this is your holiday too. Surely you don't want to be bothered with a pair of English visitors."

"It will be a pleasure," said Mahmoud. "You are staying at the Hotel El Marrak—I have read your labels, you see! That is only a few streets away from where I live."

"Well, if you are sure," said Mr Bailey, as the stewardess over the intercom wished them a pleasant holiday in Marrakesh.

"Tomorrow morning, then, at ten?" said Mahmoud.

"Why don't you join me for a drink at the hotel this evening?" said Mr Bailey. "We can plan a route for tomorrow."

"Delightful," said Mahmoud. He bowed slightly and left them.

Jenny was breathless with excitement all the way to the hotel. Some of the roads were, to her surprise, very wide and modern, and there were fast, new cars speeding along them. Using the same roads, and looking very out of place beside the cars, were donkeys pulling carts; and some of the carts were laden so high with cloth-covered packages that the entire load looked in danger of falling off.

"See how the man of the family rides on the cart while his wife trails along behind with a load on her back," said Jenny's father, "I don't think your mother would like that!"

"She'd probably say it's just like coming home from Tesco," said Jenny. "Look at those palm trees. Isn't it amazing how so many beautiful plants grow here so near the desert. Oh, is this our hotel?" It was. The coach pulled into the forecourt and Jenny and her father joined the queue to register.

"Your first time abroad?" said the elegant Arab woman behind the desk when it was their turn. Jenny nodded. "You will enjoy it." The woman smiled. "Listen—I must whisper or lose my job. Do not buy your souvenirs in the hotel shop. Much cheaper elsewhere."

Jenny grinned back. "Thanks. I'll remember."

"That was nice of her," Mr Bailey said later as he unpacked in his room. "I expect she noticed the way you were peeping in at the doorway of the shop. She's right, though. It must be cheaper if you barter for what you want in the markets."

"Oh, Dad, I won't have the nerve," giggled Jenny. "Look, there's the pool. Isn't the water blue? Can I go for a swim before we eat? Oh, Dad, isn't it marvellous? Sorry to babble on, but it's all so exciting. I'll calm down in a bit."

"The sooner the better!" laughed her father.

Mahmoud was waiting in the foyer for them when they came

Jenny was breathless with excitement all the way to the hotel

out of the hotel dining-room later that evening after dinner.

"I'm off for an early night," said Jenny. "Goodnight." As she returned to her room, Mr Bailey and Mahmoud walked into the bar. Mr Bailey smiled at the friendly receptionist as they passed the desk, but she seemed not to notice him. "Now you must tell me what is the best thing to drink here," he said.

Mahmoud shrugged. "You must take no notice of me. It is against our faith to take alcohol ... but I shall enjoy the evening as much with my lemonade as you with your whisky."

"Tomorrow," said Mr Bailey, "I hope you will take us somewhere to sample Moroccan mint tea. I hear it is delicious."

"Certainly," said Mahmoud, and so, next day, he included a visit to a café on the list of places to go.

"But to enjoy mint tea to the full, you must first become very hot," he said to Jenny, "so we will shop in the souks first, and go to the café afterwards." They spent an hour or so wandering around the tiny lanes which were packed with all kinds of wares for sale. Beggars ran after them, small boys mainly, demanding money; but when they saw that they were with Mahmoud they ran away again. Jenny bought a leather belt, punched with a pattern of hearts. It cost her several dinars more than Mahmoud said she should have paid for it, but Jenny did not care.

"I'm not very good at this bargaining yet," she said. "But I'll improve with practice."

They moved into a street where the dyers had hung their brilliant red and yellow skeins of yarn, and lengths of cloth, across the street to dry.

"What a beautiful sight," said Mr Bailey. He held a camera to his eye and would have taken a photograph, but Mahmoud stood quickly in front of him.

"First," he said, "you must bargain with the dyer for the right to photograph his wares." It took some time, but at last a smiling, well-paid dyer sat grinning in his doorway while Mr Bailey took the picture. The same thing happened when a wizened man, carrying a copper drinking-bowl with several more bowls and water-jugs clattering around his person, came into view.

"You have to pay them first," insisted Mahmoud. "They make more money this way than by actually selling anything."

"I'll remember," said Mr Bailey. "Oh, I say! Just look at those acrobats." They had come out of the narrow streets into a big open space. Not that there was any more room to walk, even so, for the whole area was a teeming mass of people. Jenny was fascinated by the jugglers and acrobats, and willingly threw some money into the collecting bowl. She hurried past the snakecharmer, though, with a shudder. Her father was horrified to see a man sitting down on a chair amid an interested crowd, to have a tooth pulled out without any kind of pain-killer.

"This is the Djemaa-el-Fna, the central square of Marrakesh, where everyone meets friends," said Mahmoud. "And now we will drink mint tea in the café over there. Upstairs, if you like, so that we can look out on everything which is going on." The café was not crowded and they found a table at the balcony edge, where they could look down on everyone. The long sprigs of mint in the glasses of hot liquid amused Jenny.

"Why, it is just like the mint in our garden at home!"

"Then you will be able to make mint tea for yourself when you return to England," said Mahmoud.

After more shopping they returned to the hotel for lunch and parted from Mahmoud at the door.

"See you tomorrow," he said. "Perhaps you would like to visit the amethyst mines in the desert, where the Berber tribesmen work? Or take a horse-drawn carriage to the camel market?"

"It will be hard to choose between them" said Jenny's father. "I think we'll make up our minds in the morning."

That afternoon, while her father snoozed in his room, Jenny took her book down to the pool's edge and swam a little, sunbathed and read a little, and drank a lot of fresh orange juice. The waiter who brought her drinks was very young, and spoke excellent English.

"I am not really on the hotel staff," he told Jenny. "My mother, you have seen, yes? She is the hotel receptionist."

"Oh, you can borrow this when I have finished reading it."

"Oh, yes," said Jenny. "She was so friendly when we arrived." She did not think it was polite to say more, but to herself she said, "And since then she has been ... well, like an enemy. As if we have done something unforgiveable. But she has never been rude, so how can I mention it?"

"I am hoping to go to university in Rabat next year," he went on. "I am learning hard to pass my exams. Especially the English one. But it is very hard for us to get English books to practise our reading." He looked pointedly at Jenny's paperback which lay on the towel beside her.

"Oh, you can borrow this when I have finished reading it," she said. "It is a good one for someone learning our language because it is for children. I have brought it with me because it has been a favourite of mine for years." The boy picked it up and studied the cover.

The Secret Garden," he said. "Is that what it is called? Me, I am called Afrim. And you?"

"Jenny."

"Jenny, I look forward to looking at your book. Thank you," smiled Afrim, and he returned to his work.

Next morning Jenny was up very early and went for a walk in the hotel gardens. Even so early in the morning of a November day the sun was blazing down, but it was shady under the palms and oleanders. Jenny wandered around for a while, and then went into the hotel foyer to read the end of her book while waiting for her father to come down to breakfast. He arrived just as she closed the book, and they ate boiled eggs and drank coffee while deciding whether to choose the amethyst mines or the camel market. They were still undecided when the meal was over and they left the dining-room.

"Well, whichever it is, I think I'll go up to my room and change this jacket for a lighter one," said Mr Bailey. "I won't be long." Jenny watched him climb the spiral staircase in the centre of the hotel foyer.

"Good morning!" came a voice from the doorway. Turning, she saw Mahmoud walking towards her. At the same time, she noticed that Afrim's mother was on duty at the desk, and that Afrim himself was striding from one doorway to another farther along the foyer. All this made a tableau in Jenny's mind, one which she was to remember later in slow motion, over and over again. At the time, nothing seemed out of the ordinary; the hotel was the most familiar part of strange, exciting Marrakesh.

"Hello, Mahmoud," she said. "Excuse me a minute—I must speak to someone." She ran forward a few steps towards Afrim, then checked herself as she realised that she was no longer holding her book.

"Afrim!" she called. He turned to her; his mother looked up.

"Have you seen *The Secret Garden?*" she called, her voice raised so that he would hear her across the length of the foyer. Afrim seemed to back away from her, shaking his head.

"No, no," he said, and disappeared through one of the doors. That's strange, thought Jenny. Well, perhaps I left it on the seat where I was sitting while I was waiting for Dad. She looked, but it was not there. Nearby was a bookstall, and it occurred to her that, had she dropped it near her seat, someone might have assumed it had fallen from the stall and placed it on one of the shelves. She scanned them all carefully, but there was no sign of it.

"There is something wrong?" asked Mahmoud. Behind him, the receptionist seemed to gasp.

"No, no—it's just—" Jenny stopped short. Her father, coming down the spiral staircase to join them, suddenly tripped and fell down the last few stairs.

"Dad! Are you all right?" Jenny rushed over to where he lay on the floor. The hotel staff and Mahmoud began to gather round. Mr Bailey struggled to his feet.

"Silly thing to do! Yes, thank you, love, I'm—ouch, no, I think I've damaged my ankle. What a wretched nuisance. Aaah! I'm sorry, Mahmoud, but I can't sightsee in this condition. You take Jenny. Try to get back for lunch, and tell me all about it." Jenny helped him back upstairs and made sure he had everything he was likely to need. Then she returned to Mahmoud.

"Well, I'm afraid the amethyst mines are out for today" she said. "Quite honestly, I'd like to go back to the souks this morning if it's all right with you. I could do some of the shopping which is most likely to bore Dad."

"As you wish," said Mahmoud, and they took a horse-drawn carriage from outside the hotel to the part of the city where the tiny shops began.

"You spent a pleasant afternoon yesterday?" Mahmoud inquired, as the horse clip-clopped his way along.

"Oh yes? I went for a swim in the pool, and read my book, and tried to get a bit of a suntan," said Jenny, smiling ruefully at the pale pink arms which went with her fair hair. "Only I don't tan very easily."

"You have not been abroad many times, I think?" continued Mahmoud. "Never to Morocco before?"

"Oh, nowhere!" said Jenny. "I'm lucky to be here now! The whole family couldn't have come, it would have cost far too much."

"Money is short, is it? You are poor?" asked Mahmoud. Jenny was shocked at such a strange question. I suppose it's because he's foreign, she thought to herself. An English person would never have asked a question like that.

"Well—no, or Dad and I wouldn't be here either," she said. "Oh look—we've arrived. I really must get some of those beads which the Berber tribesmen make."

"Do not buy the first ones you see," advised Mahmoud. "And when you know that you have found the ones you want, pretend you cannot afford them. Walk away from the stall. Then when the stall-holder calls you back with a new price, accept it. This will be his lowest offer before getting insulted."

"It's like being an actress," laughed Jenny. "Well, I'll do my best."

They walked around the stalls, and Jenny was surprised how much she remembered from the day before. There will be a kebab stall around the next bend, she would say to herself, and sure enough, when they turned the corner the steam was rising

"That is almost giving them away!" she exclaimed

from the meat which lay grilling over the charcoal embers. Mahmoud dived into the stalls from time to time to examine something at the back or perhaps to greet a friend, and Jenny, too, lingered over some stalls so long as nearly to lose sight of her guide when she came out again.

"Don't worry—we will not lose each other," laughed Mahmoud, "If we do, go to the carriage rank and take a ride back to the hotel, but it will not happen."

Between fighting off the requests for money that the half-grown children of the streets made on her, and bargaining for a good price on the beads she saw, Jenny had not much time to worry about getting lost. At last she came to a stall where the trader offered her some beautiful beads at such a low price that she felt it wrong to bargain with him at all.

"That is almost giving them away!" she exclaimed. The trader shrugged, and flashed his gold-capped teeth at her.

"True. But you have a lovely face. English, yes? I cannot bargain with a rose of England." Jenny laughed, and exchanged some coins for the beads.

"And now you will do me the honour of taking a glass of mint tea with me in the back room?" Jenny peered round the side of the stall. Mahmoud was not far way. She signalled to him that she was going farther into the stall and he waved in recognition.

"Your friend, he join us too," said the friendly trader, ushering her into a tiny room at the back, behind a curtain.

"That is very kind of you," said Jenny, noting the mint tea infusing on the stove. Then, suddenly, the man's hand was over her face, her arm was pinned behind her, and she was hastily thrust up some stairs. Struggle as she might, she could do nothing to escape the strong hold of the man who had her in his grasp. Gasping, choking, she was shoved into a room, and as the hands let her go and she fell forward, a door behind her banged and she realised that she was in total darkness. She was terrified and her instinct was to scream in panic. Calm down, Jenny, she urged herself. Think, think. Why? Mahmoud. Where was

Mahmoud? By an eerie coincidence, the same second that his name sprang to her mind, she heard his voice coming from somewhere beneath her level, calling her name.

"Jenny? Jenny! Are you hiding? Jenny!"

"I'm here! Mahmoud! The stall where you last saw me. Mahmoud!" She listened, clutching the wall in front of her, and then started to sob as, despite her cries, the sound of his voice grew fainter and fainter. He was moving along the souk in his search for her. Now he would never hear her. She'd be stuck here ... panic began to rise again in her throat, a feeling she had never experienced before, but rather like being sick. Steady, steady ... this wouldn't help. Think. Think why a strange man who you've never seen in your life should want to kidnap you. White slave trade? Don't be ridiculous. There isn't much sense in any of it, though, is there?

Jenny's finger throbbed. She sucked it, and realised that she had broken a nail in her scramble across the room. Just when she had managed to stop biting them, too, and let them grow to a more elegant length. I would take months to get that nail back to match the others.

Whatever was she thinking of, worrying about a broken nail at a time like this? The thought brought her back to reality and she began to think with amazing clarity. She had to discover a reason for this room's darkness. Rooms were not made without some sort of light. Therefore the source of it must be blocked off. She went round the walls, touching the rough plaster gingerly as she went, unsure of what she might find. Suppose there was a spider? No, she must not think of spiders. Think of light, she told herself. A window, blocked off.

She found it. A piece of board, a few millimetres thick, protruded against her fingers. More than one nail was broken before she could rip it from the wall. Almost crying, but this time with frustration, not fright, she wrestled with it. At last it tore in a jagged diagonal line, half on, half off, but giving a big enough gap for Jenny to wriggle through the window space into the blazing sunlight, to the flat roof outside. No wonder they had blocked up the window. She looked back at the hole in the wall which formed the window. They could never have held anyone prisoner in that room without blocking off the window space; but had they known she was coming? If so, how? Or was the window permanently blocked off?

She crawled to the edge of the roof and looked down. There was the back doorway to the shop, immediately below. Then she froze. Coming out of the doorway, casting a furtive glance around before diving into the throng which moved along the souk, was Afrim. Afrim! Why should he be plotting against her?

It was easy to get off the roof: one foot on a window ledge, and then a long jump to the ground. She landed safely, and looked around. Suddenly, there was Afrim again, turning back in her direction. She span round to run from him, and there, too, was Mahmoud.

"Mahmoud!" she shrieked in relief, and the tall Arab turned from the man he was talking to and gazed at her in amazement. Then Jenny noticed the man who had been talking to him. It was the trader who had locked her in.

Behind her, Afrim fought his way through the crowds to reach her. Ahead, Mahmoud was doing the same. Who could she trust? Neither of them! Quicker than thought, Jenny acted. A side lane stood invitingly near, and she dived down it. Behind her, the man and the boy called her name. Mahmoud was the one to catch her. Afrim disappeared.

"Let go! Leave me alone, you beast!"

"Jenny, Jenny!" When he had calmed her down, Mahmoud explained that he was asking the trader where she had gone. "Nothing more, I promise you. Why should I want to kidnap you?"

It seemed silly to say anything about the white slave trade. Jenny accepted his explanation and told him about Afrim.

"Yes, I saw him. He is a dangerous boy. It would be better for us to get away from here. I cannot explain why, not here, but let us not spoil the morning. Let us take a taxi to the camel market."

"Is there time?" asked Jenny. "Dad wants me back at the hotel for lunch so I can tell him where we have been."

"Ah, lunch ... well, that is, how do you say—a moveable feast," said Mahmoud. "Twelve o'clock, two o'clock—or any time in between. It would be better for you to do something interesting to get over your shock than to go back to your hotel and brood over it, no?"

"I suppose you're right," said Jenny. Certainly she could hardly bear to think of the terror she had felt, alone in that darkened room.

After a short ride, the taxi drew up at the entrance to what looked to Jenny like a field of hardened mud, in which stood a collection of mules, horses and camels.

"Oh, why do they all have one leg tied up!" exclaimed Jenny. "How cruel." Mahmoud walked beside her as they made their way round the market.

"To stop them getting away, of course," he said, casually. "They will not walk far on three legs." Jenny glanced at him. You are hard, she thought, to treat this so lightly. Suddenly she was not so sure any more that Mahmoud was a safe person to be with. There was a strange look in his eye, as if he were deep in thought about something — something involving her.

"English missy have a camel ride!" cried a large Arab man, leading over a very scruffy camel. Behind him, his wife sat suckling her baby in the mud beneath a shady tree. She was calling to him in Arabic, and he threw the occasional reply to her over his shoulder.

"What a good idea," said Mahmoud. "A camel ride would be just the thing this morning, wouldn't it, Jenny?"

An accident, thought Jenny. I could end up under the camel's feet and everyone would think it was an accident. Mahmoud could make that happen—if he wanted to.

"Not likely," she said, cheerfully. "I say, is that your baby? What a dear little thing. I must go and have a closer look." She stepped past Mahmoud and the camel, and paused briefly by the woman with her baby. As she smiled at them, she saw out of the corner of her eye that someone was running towards her. As he came closer she recognised him. It was Afrim.

All Jenny wanted to do was to get back to the hotel and her father. She made a mad dash for the exit. Mahmoud cried out, and gave chase. Turning to glance behind her, Jenny saw Afrim pull down Mahmoud in a flying tackle; a wallet fell to the ground and Afrim snatched it up. Jenny reached the exit and ran towards a waiting taxi, but someone was gasping at her shoulder, and was pushing her into the taxi.

"Afrim—you!" she shouted. "Leave me alone. I'm going back to the hotel, and you can't stop me!" Afrim threw himself into the taxi beside her and leaned forward to the driver.

"Hotel El Marrak, please—quickly," he said. Then he turned to Jenny. "Don't worry—you are safe now," he said.

Jenny said nothing. She gripped the edge of her seat and looked anxiously ahead. At last the taxi drew up in front of the hotel. Jenny ran straight in, leaving Afrim to pay, but he was soon in the foyer behind her. Jenny went towards the stairs but Afrim held her back.

"Please," he said. "We must see the manager. At once."

"Oh, there I agree with you," said Jenny, angrily. "I have several complaints to make. About you, for one!"

"Keep your voice down," hissed Afrim. "There are things going on you know nothing of … now just follow me." He led the way to the manager's office, knocked, and went in.

"Yes, Afrim?" said the manager. He frowned at Jenny. "Excuse me, Miss Bailey, but guests…"

"Miss Bailey is here for a purpose," said Afrim, "and there is no time to lose. In exactly," he glanced at the clock on the office wall, "ten minutes members of a drug ring will attempt to make a pick-up from the bookshop in the foyer. It is imperative that the police be called to the hotel before this happens. No, I am not out of my mind, sir, I can prove it. But please call the police first, or they may be too late." Astounded, the manager nevertheless reached for the telephone. Within a few minutes members of the Moroccan police force were in the building.

"Jenny, you must stay here," said Afrim. "I will send in my mother too, for it is not safe for either of you to be in the hotel

Astounded, the manager nevertheless reached for the telephone

foyer until this is all over. She will tell you more."

Afrim's mother brought with her some cool drinks and while they sat drinking them, told Jenny as much as she knew.

"My Afrim, he trailed you this morning. I told him, do not risk your life, but he would go. For my sake, you see." Jenny did not see, and said so.

"Mahmoud has been blackmailing me. One day while I am on duty, a man comes into the hotel foyer. 'I have a parcel to deliver to the bookshop,' he tells me, 'but it is shut. Please would you take it from me and give it to the bookstall keeper when he opens?' So of course I do ... and then one day soon after, Mahmoud comes back and tells me that he will be leaving a package with me for a certain gentleman to collect. I know Mahmoud is not always as honest as he should be so I refuse ... and then he tells me that I have already helped smuggle drugs and that he will involve me up to my neck."

"How terrible!" said Jenny.

"Then he comes to the hotel all the time—every day, to see you and your father. Three days now ... I think you must be involved, but Afrim says you are innocent. So I see Mahmoud is using you, and I ask myself why? And I listen. I hear the bookshop man give a time, and a place ... which is now. There is to be another lift of books—"

"Books?" asked the puzzled Jenny. "Are the drugs hidden in the bookstall?"

"Ah, yes," said Afrim's mother. "In false books ... just the fronts and backs, with holes cut in the middles and the drugs stuffed in. Then all wrapped in cellophane to look like new. So I see, Mahmoud needs an excuse to be waiting in the foyer every day. What can be more natural than he should look at the bookstall, chat to the man there, while he waits for you? Then you do something very silly. You ask my Afrim if he has seen The Garden."

"I do what?" said Jenny. "Oh—you mean *The Secret Garden?*"

"Yes—that is the name of the drug gang's headquarters—I have found that out," said Afrim's mother. "And you go to the

"She offered me a fabulous sum of money for this paperback."

bookstall and start peering around. I think you have gone mad. And Mahmoud is all the time watching you, like an eagle."

"But—I was only looking for my paperback," said Jenny.

"Afrim, he tell me that afterwards," went on Afrim's mother. "But at the time, it look sinister. Mahmoud, he obviously think you know about his drug racket. So Afrim go to follow you when you leave with Mahmoud."

Jenny was just going to ask if her father was all right when the door opened and Afrim came in.

"We caught them all in the act," he said, smiling, "and they had already caught Mahmoud in the camel market, looking for his wallet, which I had all the time," he went on. "It contained a lot of incriminating evidence."

"But why," said Jenny, "did they lock me up in that room?" Afrim's mother gasped.

"They did that? Oh—"

"It's all right," said Afrim. "It would take more than a blocked-up window to keep Jenny in. You had to be kept out of the hotel past lunchtime. They were afraid you knew enough to see what was going on."

"And when that failed, Mahmoud took me to the camel market to kill some more time," said Jenny. "I see!"

Up in his room, Mr Bailey was feeling very bored.

"Fancy being laid up on holiday," he said, as his daughter walked in. "The highspot of my morning has been a chat with the chambermaid. Do you know, she offered me a fabulous sum of money for this paperback. It seems they can't get enough of them in this country. Talking of paperbacks, I found yours in here. I must have taken it up with my jacket after breakfast." Jenny sank down on the nearest chair and wondered what to tell him first.

"You know, Jenny, we could start a good racket smuggling paperbacks into Morocco," said Mr Bailey. "I say—I'm only joking, you know! Jenny—why are you laughing like that?"

"Oh Dad!" laughed Jenny. "If you only knew! Make yourself comfortable and I'll tell you what I did this morning."

In Focus

by GEOFFREY MORGAN

Soon after midnight Sue Harvey awoke and shook her companion. The howl of the wind outside the tent was enough to waken a hibernating dormouse; but it did not disturb Jean Marsden. Tired after their long day's cycle ride, she slept soundly.

"Jean—Jean!" Sue called, shaking her friend's shoulder. "The wind's playing havoc outside. I think some of the pegs have worked loose." Sue slipped her anorak over her pyjamas. "You'll have to come out and hold the torch while I batten down." Jean sat up, rubbing her eyes. "Get your anorak on and bring the torch." She picked up the mallet, unfastened the tent flap and stepped outside.

The night wind was cold off the North Sea though summer was not yet over, and across the moonless sky lowering clouds hid the stars. Behind the tent the copse rose up gloomy and sombre, the branches of the trees gesticulating wildly against the invisible force blowing through them. At the bottom of the grassy slope ran the lane to the village, and beyond that the marshland and creeks melted into the sea. Somewhere to the left of their camp, on the sharp rise overlooking a meandering creek, stood the the keep and battlements of Longford Castle.

The two friends were enjoying a camping holiday in Suffolk. Sue, the elder, was tall and fair. Jean was slim and dark haired.

Their bicycles gave them an independence that took them on from place to place unless a particular location held some special attraction for them when they would stay more than the customary one night. The sleepy coastal village of Longford with its many sheltered stretches of water, its pleasure boats and fishing craft and its variety of birdlife, held just that special attraction, particularly for Sue for she was a keen photographer.

It was only a matter of minutes to attend to the pegs and guy-ropes; but before re-entering the tent their attention was attracted by a slowly-moving light in the vicinity of the castle.

"That's strange," murmured Sue. "Who'd be moving around that desolate spot at this hour?" Sue stared through the darkness. "It's someone moving down to the creek. Whoever it is must have been up to the castle keep."

They stood there watching as the light vanished and reappeared, obscured one moment by trees or bushes or the undulations of the ground and revealed again the next as it cleared these obstacles on its way to the water's edge.

Sue, unable to contain her curiosity, moved down the slope from the camp to where the ground rose again in a shallow hillock. She lay down in the rough grass, peering over the top, and a few moments later Jean reluctantly joined her. In the darkness it was difficult to distinguish land from water. The creek was a faint outline of a lighter pattern running though the dark mass of the land. A shadowy finger at the tide's edge Sue identified as the old jetty they had seen when they arrived. The light was there now and then suddenly it was extinguished.

"Listen!" Sue whispered. On the wind they heard the creak and splash of oars. "Whoever it is is now rowing a dinghy." She looked at her companion. "What would he have wanted at the castle?"

"You tell me," Jean said, suppressing a shiver. "Let's get back to the tent. I'm frozen!"

Sue did not move. She was peering into the darkness again. The sound of the dinghy had faded and died but further down the creek she was sure the still shadow she could discern on the water was a yacht, or it may have been a fishing boat. Was that where the dinghy had gone?

Jean got up. "Come on. Whatever's afoot, it's all over now." Sue followed her slowly back to the tent.

"It might be just the beginning," she said.

They were up early to find that the wind had dropped and the morning was calm and warm with the sun climbing up into a cloudless sky. Even the forbidding architecture of the castle keep looked mellow and harmless in the still air.

The creek running up beside the castle was an isolated waterway with a wide expanse of marsh on either side, and since it led nowhere except to the castle it was not used by local boatmen. It was a quiet anchorage for any visiting yachts, but the only boat there now was a large white ketch. It lay downstream of the old jetty in the middle of the channel, and Sue was sure it represented the shadow they had discerned the night before.

"Well," Jean announced as they put away the breakfast dishes. "I suppose the first thing we do is look at the castle."

"No." Sue was smiling as she collected her camera. "That comes later. The first thing is to take a look at that yacht."

"At the yacht?" Jean queried. She knew Sue's weakness for boats. Her brother sometimes took her sailing; but she suspected that her friend was interested in something more than just the craft itself. "But you won't get a better view of the boat than from here."

"We will from another boat," Sue returned dryly. "I'd like to get some close-up pictures. We'll hire a boat in the village."

Longford was a small straggling village, its one street ending in a large square near the creek. There was a post office and general store facing each other across the square with about half a dozen timbered cottages on either side of them. They found the boatyard at the end of a sandy lane, and within ten minutes they were afloat in a brightly varnished dinghy.

"I'll row," Sue said, confidently. "It can't be far."

It was further than she thought, however. Castle Creek, as the boatman called it when Sue inquired, ran off the main channel

The only boat there now was a large white ketch

beyond a tree-lined point a kilometre down from the boatyard. The tide was about half-flood and Sue kept close to the shore to avoid the mainstream. Once they rounded the point the tide was with them and soon they were in Castle Creek.

Jean had a good view of the castle from the boat. Although it stood above the creek it was lower and much nearer the water than she had thought. It was built on a shallow rise with a riot of stunted trees and bushes around its base, and patches of sandstone and large boulders mostly covered with scrub overlaid the slope right down to the water's edge.

"See anyone aboard the yacht?" Sue asked.

"Hmm," Jean nodded. "A big man, bald, just come up from below. I can just see his head now," Jean went on in a low voice. "He's looking at us through binoculars." A few moments later, "Now he's disappeared."

The gap between the dinghy and the yacht slowly narrowed, and when they were abeam Sue shipped the oars.

She was a yacht of some 13 metres in length with a wooden hull and two tall masts. She had wide decks and a shallow deckhouse with a companionway opening into the cockpit aft. A dinghy was hitched astern; but the craft lay so quiet with her deck and cockpit now deserted, she might have been abandoned. Sue edged the dinghy closer and started clicking her camera shutter. Suddenly a tall slim man in a peaked cap appeared and came to the rail.

"Do you mind keeping clear!" His voice was low with a hint of anger. "The topsides have just been painted. I don't want any damage."

"I am keeping clear," Sue called back pleasantly. "We were just admiring her."

"I mean well clear!" the man retorted, his anger obvious now. "The tide will sweep you into us where you are."

Sue said nothing. She began pulling away and the man disappeared below. As they passed the yacht's stern they could read her name on the counter: *Misty Dawn.* Below there were some faint letters which could have spelled the port of registry, but they had been painted over. In any case, after the unpleasant reception they dare not go close enough to identify them.

"Wasn't exactly a welcome, was it?" Jean murmured.

"What did you expect?" Sue returned, her voice edged with excitement, "if they've got something to hide. There's something going on. The first man disappearing after squinting at us through the glasses; the other man trying to scare us away and the port of registry unreadable. I'm sure there's some link now between the yacht and the castle."

"So the castle's next?" suggested Jean, her throat dry with tense anticipation as she realised that her friend's first suspicions of some mystery now appeared to be confirmed.

"I can't get there fast enough," was Sue's excited comment.

Early that afternoon they were ascending the wide track that led to the main entrance of the castle keep. Once through the doorway they found themselves in a narrow stone passage that turned twice before opening into a large circular hall which had, in the more recent past, huge bow windows built into the thick wall. A uniformed figure rose from the small table on one side, and came towards them as they stood looking round.

"Good afternoon." The man's thin lips twisted into a smile of welcome. The girls cheerfully returned his greeting. "Admission is twenty-five pence to students," he said, "and includes this brief history and a plan of the original castle."

As soon as they had paid their money the warden lost interest in them, returning to his chair by the window, and the two girls hurried into the central broad passageway and began working their way up the circular stone stairs.

Certainly there was little on the surface to interest them since they were not seeking to investigate the castle's history as much as the more recent events on their minds; but they found nothing to suggest any connection with the mysterious light they had seen the night before or with the yacht. There were just a few dark closets and small airless chambers, and a confusing number of twisting passages that seemed to lead nowhere in particular. Many ended in a blank wall while others

Instinctively, they were cautious

broadened out into small cell-like rooms with arrow-slits in the walls. The only reward for climbing all the stone steps was the extensive views up and down the coast from the battlements, and the first object they focused on was the yacht.

"The dinghy's gone," Sue said, her gaze moving across the water to the jetty. "It doesn't look as if anyone has come ashore down there. They may have gone to the village."

Sue began taking shots of the surrounding scenery. Immediately below them and adjoining the keep the crumbling outer wall of the castle revealed nothing within except a few ancient foundations overrun with grass, and Sue took a shot of this before they moved back inside and descended the stairs.

When they reached the level directly above the main hall Jean paused. "Are you going to say anything to the warden about the light we saw?" she whispered.

Sue shook her emphatically. "Not a word to anyone."

They descended to the ground floor, but before they reached the hall, they heard voices. Instinctively, they were cautious, Sue peering round the corner of the stonework into the hall. She drew back instantly, whispering to Jean, "I'm sure it's the man from the yacht. The bald-headed man—take a peep!"

Jean looked scared, but her quick glance confirmed the identification. "That's the one. He had the binoculars on us."

"Listen!" Sue whispered; and in the silence the bald man's voice was loud enough for them to catch some of his words.

"...telephoned from the village ... There was some hold-up ... looks clear now ... Many visitors? ..."

"A couple of students ... up on top somewhere ..."

There was a long pause and then, "What about the sign? Did you fix it?" It was the bald man talking.

"I've been meaning to. I'll do it now." The men began to move towards the passage and Sue turned, pulling Jean after her. Hurrying silently along the corridor, they turned into the first dark recess. This became another passage with an oak door at the end. Hanging down from the centre panel of the door held askew by one nail was a notice: *Private. No Admittance.*

They instantly realised that this was the notice the men were coming to fix. Sue tried the door and it creaked inward. She stared down at a flight of stone steps. Next moment both girls were on the steps and had pulled the door closed after them. They heard the men outside and then some brief tapping with a hammer as nails were driven through the notice board into the door. In the ensuing silence they heard the men's footsteps retreating until they died away altogether.

"Whatever the mystery is the warden seems to be in on it," Jean observed in a hushed voice.

Sue was nodding. "That notice has something to do with it, too. Keeping the public out of here. Let's go and have a look."

Jean followed with some reluctance. The air was musty and the rough stonework of the walls was clammy to their touch as they supported themselves on the steps. Although it was darker than any other part of the keep, rays of light penetrated from some hidden ventilator. At the bottom of the flight of steps was a door. The bolt slipped back silently as if it had been recently oiled. Sue pushed open the door and they stepped into a large square room. A shaft of sunlight filtered through a square hole in the outside wall revealing a rough stone floor. The scarred walls were broken only by a heavy oak door centred in the outside wall. Sue crossed to the aperture which formed a glassless square window. The lower sill was just below shoulder height, and she leaned out. Outside it was no more than a metre to the ground, which sloped away in a tumble of vegetation to the creek. She was surprised to find how close this part of the keep was to the water, with the old jetty not more than fifty metres away. A snaking depression in the grass formed a track that led towards the water's edge, and Sue was just about to raise her camera to take a shot when Jean called her over to the door.

"Take a look," she said. "The door's locked, but the bolt slides easily enough."

Sue examined it, nodding. "Oiled, like the other one. It looks like a well trodden track outside leading down to the jetty. Who uses the door do you think?"

Jean was looking round. "But there's nothing here—" She suddenly broke off, moving into one of the shadowy corners of the chamber. "Hey! See this, Sue," she whispered. "It looks like a trap door."

Sue had opened the leaflet and was studying the small-scale plan of the keep. She moved to her friend's side and stared down at the square of dark timber sunk level with the floor. The hinges at one end looked black with oil.

"According to the plan this seems to have been one of the store rooms," she said, "so just below could be the dungeons."

"Dungeons! Urgh!" Jean suppressed a shiver. Sue was looking up at the thick oak beam that ran the length of the ceiling; directly above the trap a large hook was embedded in the beam.

"That hook looks like a recent addition," she observed. "What's the idea, I wonder?" She bent down. "Let's lift the trap." They each grasped one of the rings and pulled upwards. The trap rose easier than they had expected, revealing a dark square opening; but without a torch it was impossible to see how deep the shaft was. A cold, musty smell assaulted their nostrils, and just below the surface on one side of the shaft a metal gleam caught their eye. Sue sank to her knees and her hand groped for the metal. "It's a ladder," she announced, rising. "But see, on the other side, the remains of stone steps. They must have crumbled away, so the only way down is a ladder."

"You mean—someone's using the dungeons now?" Jean murmured. "I wonder..." Jean broke off. "Listen!" Footsteps could just be heard in the silence.

"It's the warden!" whispered Sue, desperately. "Quick! Close the trap." She swung round, bending low to grab the ring in such panic that the strap attached to her camera slithered down her arm and before she could prevent it her camera had disappeared down the shaft.

"Your camera!" Jean cried under her breath.

"We can't do anything now. Get this shut—*quietly!*" They closed the trap without a sound and Sue pulled her friend hurriedly towards the window as the warden appeared at the door.

"Can't you girls read?" he demanded angrily. They turned towards him and Sue said calmy, "Read what?"

"The notice on the door up there," he pointed up the stairs.

"I'm sorry, but we didn't see any notice," she apologised. "We were just exploring. Nothing wrong in that, is there?"

"The public aren't allowed down her." His voice was firm but the anger had drained away. "It's dangerous. There's restoration work to be done in these lower chambers. Perhaps you would now return to the hall." He suddenly stared at Sue. "Didn't you have a camera, young lady?"

"Yes, and we were just coming up to get it." Sue spoke calmly and went on to lie without hesitation. "I was leaning out to get a shot through the window there," she nodded at the aperture, "caught my elbow on the rough stone and dropped the camera. It landed in the grass outside. I hope it's not damaged."

"You might have damaged yourselves down here," he said, curtly, and stood aside so that they preceded him up the steps. He closed the door and walked up after them, closing and bolting the door at the top, pointing to the notice.

"I'm sorry to have caused you any trouble," Sue said, sweetly, and they walked on to the main hall, then without another word hurried outside. "Let's go round and find the door and window just in case he's watching."

They moved round from the main entrance, negotiating a path through shrubs and sprawling bramble bushes, following the wall of the keep on the creek side until they crossed the rough track that led to the door and came up to the window.

"Pretend you're looking in the grass," she said, staring down at the undergrowth herself. After a few moments she picked up a large dark stone, half-concealing it in the crook of her arm. "Come on, from a distance this'll look as if we've found the camera. Let's get out of here."

As they approached the tent, Sue threw the stone away. "I think we got away with the act, don't you?"

"Well, I saw no sign of the warden. But what are you going to do about your camera?" asked Jean.

"Go in and get it, of course," Sue returned confidently. "When the old man has closed up and gone."

"What—down in the dungeon!" exclaimed Jean, horrified.

"If that's where it is. It won't be much different from the store room. A bit darker, maybe, but we'll have our torches. Besides," she went on, "I think we might find the link between the castle and the yacht down there."

"I don't fancy it. Why don't we go to the police?"

"What would we tell them? We've proof of nothing, and if there's nothing down there we'd just be taken for silly school kids; but if we go down and see—well, at least I'll get my camera back." She opened the tent. "Now, how about some tea?"

Over tea Jean studied the leaflet on the castle, and while Sue washed up and packed away the crockery, she read snatches of the description aloud. After a thoughtful silence she looked up at her companion. "Sue, did you read this about the dungeons?"

"What about them?"

"Well, in the old days prisoners were drowned in them. It seems that each dungeon had a large drain, and before some of the land around here was reclaimed from the sea and the marshes, the tides came up almost to the base of the keep on one side, like a kind of one-sided moat. Anyway, these drains fed into it but when the tide rose the water came up the drain into the dungeons and drowned the victims imprisoned there."

"That doesn't surprise me. In those days there were far worse tortures than drowning. Come on, now," she encouraged. "Stop giving yourself the creeps, and get ready. The warden shuts up shop in about half an hour, and I want to see him go."

Twenty minutes later, as the evening sun was topping the horizon, they were settled just below a ridge from where they had the main entrance of the keep in view. From their position they also had the yacht under observation, but there was no movement on deck and the dinghy still trailed astern. Eventually, they saw the warden leave and, after waiting another ten minutes, they left their hiding-place and headed for the keep.

Once below the aperture Sue got Jean to give her a leg-up

Jean joined her friend in a small stone chamber

and a moment she was through the opening and leaning down, hauling up her companion. With the torches glowing, they soon had the trap door open and the shaft flooded with light. The ladder went down about five metres to an uneven stone base at the bottom. The camera was lying on some old sacking.

"There!" Sue whispered excitedly. "No wonder I didn't hear it land!" She swung round on to the top rung of the ladder. "Here goes!" she murmured cheerfully, and went slowly down. Jean remained above, watching. She saw Sue pick up the camera.

"No damage," she called up, and then Jean saw her shine the torch into an opening on the opposite side to the ladder.

"Come down and look," Sue said. "It looks as if someone's using the dungeon in a very different way than the bad old barons of the past."

Jean descended reluctantly, joining her friend in a small stone chamber in which were stacked about a dozen wooden cases. Sue moved forward to examine one. There were no identifying marks. She drew a penknife from her pocket, opened the spike and began to prise at one of the battens. The end eventually split and pulling back the strips of wood and a mass of straw, she lifted out a bottle. She flashed her torch over it.

"Brandy!" she whispered. "So it's a smuggler's nest!"

"Landed from the yacht..." Jean murmured. "But why dump it here?"

"To await collection."

"Of course—don't you remember? The talk we overheard. The bald man from the yacht told the warden he had telephoned from the village. He said there'd been some hold-up but it looked all clear now," said Jean. "But why should he wait in the creek if he's done his part and unloaded?"

"Perhaps he's waiting for his money."

"Well, we've found the link. Let's go and tell the police."

"Just a minute." Sue was flashing her torch low down along one wall. "Look—that old metal cover." She bent down, pulling at one side and it swung back revealing a large circular opening. "This must be one of the drains you were talking about."

"I'll take your word for it. Let's go!" Sue followed her into the shaft and Jean started to climb the ladder. She had not gone up more than half a dozen rungs when she suddenly froze. The distant banging of a door seeped down to her.

"Someone's up there!" she gasped. "Did you hear it?"

"Yes. Come down." As Jean reached the bottom there came the sound of men's voices, then distant footsteps.

"Quick!" Sue urged. "And keep the light down." She led Jean back into the dungeon. "The drain," she whispered. "It's our only way out now."

"But supposing it's blocked?" They heard an angry voice shout, "The trap's been left open!"

Sue pushed Jean forward. "Go on—we're trapped. Get into the drain. They'll be down in seconds." Jean crawled in and Sue pulled the metal cover over the entrance leaving enough space to squeeze herself through. She switched off her torch, told Jean to shield her beam just sufficiently to show the way ahead, and they began crawling slowly away from the sound of the voices.

It seemed like an eternity before the scent of fresh air obliterated the damp, stuffy atmosphere of the circular tunnel that at times appeared so confined they had difficulty in scraping through. After several pauses Sue called to Jean to switch off the torch for a moment. When she did they could see, some way ahead, a small circle that was lighter than the pitch blackness of their surroundings.

A little later they were crawling out into the night air through a screen of brambles. They stood for a moment, breathing deeply and stretching their stiff limbs. The stars were shining but a mist was creeping up the creek from the sea. Sue led the way down to the jetty not more than a few metres away. She stood there looking over the deserted waterway.

"The yacht's gone," she said.

"We can't do anything about that," Jean retorted. "Let's go and wake up the village constable."

They set off, heading over rough undulating ground towards the lane. As they crested a rise on the other side of the castle they saw lights and heard voices. There was the sound of a car. Then another. In the car lights and beams of torches they could see several moving figures. They ran down the slope then up to the lane.

"It's the police!" Sue exclaimed. "Come on." The two girls, their faces scratched and dirty, their clothes torn, stumbled towards the police car, and torches were flashed over them.

"We've just come from the castle—the dungeon," Sue blurted out. "We found the smugglers' hideaway."

Safe in a police car, Sue and Jean related their story to the Inspector from the moment they entered the castle.

"Well," he murmured in admiration when he had heard them out. "You've shown some courage and initiative."

"But how did you come to be here?" asked Sue.

"Tip-off," the Inspector smiled. "We've been trying to trace the gang for some time. We arrived soon after that land-rover over there. We caught some of them red-handed moving the stuff to the castle: stolen goods, small antiques, silverware to be lodged in the keep before being shipped to the continent."

"But we thought they were smuggled goods—brandy and—"

"That's right," the Inspector nodded. "It's a sort of two-way traffic. Goods were brought in from Holland and the French ports, and hauls in this country were taken out; but we haven't any information yet on the vessel used."

"It's a yacht," Sue said. "A wooden ketch. She was lying in the creek earlier this evening. Her name is *Misty Dawn*."

"The name will have been changed by now, and this sea mist is coming in. Can you give me any further details?"

"I can do better than that." Sue held up her camera. "I've got shots of the boat from every angle in here."

"Well, that's a master-stroke," he beamed, then called to one of his men. "There's a film in this camera I want processed immediately. You won't mind us borrowing it," the Inspector said. I'll see you get more than your film back."

Sue looked up and smiled. "I don't mind," she said, "as long as you do me some enlargements!"

The Camargue Encounter

by SALLY TAYLOR

"Look!" cried Jean-Pierre suddenly, standing up in his stirrups. "Look over there! Can you see the white stallion on the top of the hill? I wonder why he is so agitated—let's go and see what is happening." With that, he sat down in the saddle and was off at a gallop, leaving the others to follow.

Christopher and Susan Marshall were spending their Easter holidays in southern France with some friends of their parents, Monsieur and Madame Runier, who had a farm close to St Gilles, in the heart of the Camargue. Already they were loving it; they loved the French farmhouse with its bright wallpaper and stone floors; they loved the marshy countryside with its tall, green reeds and silvery-blue, meandering waterways and they loved the fact that Monsieur and Madame Runier had two children, Jean-Pierre and Michelle, who were just about the same age as they were. Best of all they loved the horses—those belonging to their hosts, certainly, because they could ride them: but they loved it too, when they caught glimpses of the wild horses that roamed, proud and free, over the plains of the Camargue.

M. Runier had told them all about the wild white horses their first night at dinner. They had been sitting at the scrubbed, wooden table in the kitchen, tucking into huge platefuls of cassoulet and chunks of crusty French bread. M. Runier told them how the horses had lived in the region long before man arrived, having, it was believed, descended from prehistoric horses. Although their coats were nearly always some shade of grey, the foals were born black. Their coats became progressively whiter as they got older.

"They love their freedom, the Camargue horses, just like the Camargue people," M. Runier mused, puffing on his pipe now. "And the stallions will protect their mares and offspring against all intruders or possible enemies. The foals are quite young at the moment, so the stallions will be on the lookout for trouble. Give them a wide berth if you see them while you are out riding, won't you?"

For the first few days of their holiday, the children had not gone for very long rides. They would go for a couple of hours or so in the morning, returning to the farmhouse for lunch. In the afternoon, Jean-Pierre would take them down the waterways of the Camargue, steering the narrow boat deftly along the canals with a long pole. It was then, if they went far enough into the marshes, that they would sometimes see small herds of wild horses. Usually they were just grazing peacefully, the young foals nuzzling their mothers' sides eagerly. Against the calm, clear blue skies that are an almost legendary feature of the Camargue, it was the most perfect sight that Susan and Christoher had ever seen.

That evening, when they got back to the farmhouse, Jean-Pierre anounced that he had planned a full day's riding expedition for the next day. "We'll take a picnic lunch with us and really explore."

It was hard to go to sleep that night, but once the warm sun began to push through the curtains in the early morning, any further hope of slumber was out of the question. After breakfast, the children ran outside to catch and groom the ponies.

Jean-Pierre and Michelle's ponies came trotting over at the sound of the children's calls and the rattling of the bucket. The two that Christopher and Susan had been riding followed close

They found a cool spot in the shade of some low, bushy trees

behind. All the ponies had Camargue blood in them, although the gleaming chestnut coat of Jean-Pierre's Folco, and the patchy skewbald markings of the little mare, Claire, that Susan was riding, indicated that their blood was not pure. Christopher's pony, Lancier, was not grey either, but had a shiny, black coat. Michelle, however, was riding her beloved Ballerine, a beautiful dappled grey with a thick mane, flowing tail and finely chiselled features.

At last the ponies' coats were brushed, their tails tangle-free and their hooves glistening with the hoof oil that had been brushed over each one. Attached to each saddle was a small pack containing the riders' lunches, while Jean-Pierre had a pack on his back, too, out of which protruded the pointed ends of two French loaves.

"Hurry up," he said to Christopher, who was adjusting a strap on Lancier's bridle, "or the day'll be half done before we go!"

They begun their ride, travelling first along the paths they knew, through small clumps of trees, then along hard, mud-packed tracks that provided a solid footing through the marshes. They waved to the fishermen who were pulling up their nets to inspect the night's catch, or baling out the water from the bottom of their boats with a rusty bucket. Every now and then, the children would let their ponies splash through the fetlock-deep, cool, sparkling waters and then they would lean sideways from the saddle and watch their reflections circling outwards in the ripples beneath.

Soon after midday, they were ready for lunch. They found a cool spot in the shade of some low, bushy trees and tethered the ponies on long ropes to graze. Then they tucked into the French bread, cheeses and cold meat that Mme Runier had packed.

"I think we should copy the gardiens, the 'cowboys' of the Camargue, and have a siesta," said Jean-Pierre. He insisted, despite the protests of the others, as it was too hot for the ponies, and in spite of themselves, all four of them soon fell into a doze.

"Who didn't want to sleep then?" was the next thing they heard, and Christopher, Susan and Michelle sat up to see Jean-

Pierre standing by Folco, ready to mount. Quick as a flash, the ponies were saddled and untethered and they were ready for action.

Now they were in unknown territory, and it was when they were half an hour into the afternoon's ride that Jean-Pierre spotted the stallion on the skyline.

It took Christopher, Susan and Michelle no time at all to pick up their reins and follow Jean-Pierre's trail, but they had only been following him for a few minutes, when they saw him galloping back down the track towards them.

"What did you…" Chistopher asked, reining Lancier to a halt, but Jean-Pierre was signalling to them to be quiet.

"There are some gypsy horse thieves just over the hill," he said, softly. "They are quite common this time of year; sometimes they come to steal the mares, but these are after the foals. They've got two cornered in a make-shift corral, and they are trying to lasso a third. That's why the stallion is so agitated!"

"What shall we do?" asked Susan. "Shall we ride for help?"

Michelle shook her head. "They will be gone with the foals if we do that," she said. "Besides, we don't know where to get help. No, we must do something ourselves. Come on, think." The boys were already doing just that and in a minute they had worked out a plan.

"Michelle," Jean-Pierre directed, "you must distract the thieves somehow—pretend Ballerine's gone lame, you have lost your way, hurt yourself—anything, but try to draw them away from the corral. Susan, you come with Christopher and me. We'll get as close as we can to the corral, then Christopher can hold our ponies, I'll let the foals out of the corral, and you creep round to where the thieves' horses are tied and set them free. That way, the thieves can't ride after us. As soon as you hear me shout, Michelle, jump on to Ballerine and ride after us!"

The plan sounded simple enough and they all knew what they had to do, but even so, each one of them felt their mouth go dry with sudden fear as they rode quietly behind Jean-Pierre. Soon his hand went up, motioning them to stop.

"Okay everybody. The corral is just behind that scrubby bush. Off you go Michelle. We'll stay here out of sight until the coast is clear."

"Good luck," Susan managed to whisper and Michelle winked at her as she gathered up her reins. A minute or two later the others heard Michelle crying, "Help, please help! I think my pony has gone lame." They heard the thieves gasp in surprise. Then a rough voice said, "We'd better go and see. We don't want her to come over here. Come on—quickly."

The sound of heavy feet pushing through the undergrowth was the cue the other three had been waiting for. "Come on," whispered Jean-Pierre, kicking Folco forwards. A minute or two later, he was jumping from the pony's back. "That's far enough. Give Claire to Christopher, Susan, and follow me." Christopher took the three pairs of reins and talked softly to the horses.

Meanwhile Jean-Pierre and Susan ran as quickly and quietly as they could, keeping low so they could not be seen. They reached the corral where the young foals where whinnying— frantic and frightened. Just a little way off, the two mares were calling back to their offspring, throwing their heads upwards in anxiety, but they dared not come any nearer to the thieves' cruel lasso.

"There are their horses," Jean-Pierre whispered to Susan, pointing to where a couple of skinny horses were tethered to a bush. "Go and untie them. I'll let the foals out of here and the thieves' horses are bound to gallop away after the herd."

Almost before Susan reached the horses, Jean-Pierre had released the bottom rail of the corral "gate". A second later, the top one was out too, and the foals had raced out to join their whinnying mothers. That was Jean-Pierre's mistake—he had been too quick!

The sound of the tiny pounding hooves reached the thieves' ears, and with a shout, they had abandoned Michelle and were running back to the corral. Poor Susan had untied one horse, but was still wrestling with the stiff rope of the other's bridle, when she felt rough hands clasped against her shoulders.

He rushed at one of the thieves

"You little minx," snarled the rough gypsy face looking down at her. He gave her an angry shaking, then sneered. "Well, are your friends going to come and rescue you now, I wonder!"

Michelle had leapt on to Ballerine's back, and galloped over to join the boys. They too had mounted, and Christopher was still holding Claire's reins. "What shall we do?" Michelle asked despairingly.

"We may not need to do anything," said Jean-Pierre. "Look."

Christopher and Michelle let their gaze follow his pointing finger. Charging down towards the spot where the horse thieves were standing with Susan, was the wild white stallion. In a cloud of dust, he came thundering to a halt, his iron hooves rooted into the ground. But he was still for a second only; with a piercing neigh, he reared up, his front hooves flailing the air just in front of the thieves' tethered horse. Echoing the wild stallion's cry, it pulled violently backwards, snapping its bridle like a piece of cotton thread, and as the stallion got ready to rear again, it wheeled round and galloped away.

The three children watched, terrified but exhilarated, as the stallion trotted round in a small circle, nostrils flaring and head tossing. Then with his ears pressed hard back against his neck, he rushed at one of the thieves. Before the terrified man had time to move, the stallion had grasped his shirt in his teeth. With an upward toss of his head, the shirt sleeve was in tatters.

"You brute," screamed the thief. Then, seeing the stallion preparing to advance again, he pushed Susan to one side and ran, calling to his mate, "Come on, the beast means to kill us!"

His friend needed no second bidding and dived into the scrubby undergrowth. Susan, stunned and frightened, was sitting on the ground, where she had landed after the thief's rough treatment. The stallion stood still for a moment, towering above her and looking down at her, then he pivoted round and galloped away to join his mares.

Christopher was off Lancier's back in seconds and racing over to where Susan lay on the ground. "Sue," he panted, "are you all right? Where does it hurt?"

"Nowhere much," Susan managed a smile. "Yes, I'm all right, or I will be in a minute. Wasn't he magnificent—that stallion?"

"Do you feel ready to ride, Susan?" asked Jean-Pierre. "I think we should get out of here quickly. Once those thieves have recovered from their fright, they'll probably come back looking for us." The thought of such horror was enough to get Susan on her feet and into Claire's saddle straight away.

"Which way?" cried Michelle, looking around her uneasily.

"Follow the wild horses," cried Jean-Pierre, already spurring Folco on towards their trail. All together, they raced after the cloud of yellow dust ahead that they knew must be the fleeing horses. Not one of the four could have told you why they were following the horses and certainly not where they were going. The adventure had given them all a shock and their single thought was to get as far away as possible from the rough, and possibly dangerous, gypsy thieves.

On they rode across the sparse salt flats, sometimes splashing through shallow waters sending up great showers of crystal water drops. They hung on grimly as the ponies weaved in and out of the low scrubby bushes, and they merely winced when a branch struck across them, stinging like a whiplash.

Before long, the wild horses slowed their frenzied gallop into a more even canter, and the children let their ponies ease up too. Now they began to wonder where they were, but still they kept the wild horses in sight.

Eventually, Jean-Pierre reined Folco to a halt and the others did the same. Both ponies and riders were puffing hard and were glad to stop. The children looked around them; in front of them the ground sloped away and they could see, in the valley below, the glistening and glittering of a silver, snaking river. Beyond it, the marshes stretched endlessly into the distance. The wild horses had stopped by the river and were having a much-needed drink.

"Do you have any idea where we are, Jean-Pierre?" Susan asked hesitantly. He did not answer for a minute, but stared intently into the distance, concentrating hard.

"Follow the wild horses," cried Jean-Pierre

"Yes and no," he said finally. "Do you see that tiny cottage on the other side of the river? I'm as sure as I can be that it belongs to the fisherman, Antoine. If I'm right, I know the way home from there. What I am not so sure of, is how to cross the river."

Christopher and Susan tried hard not to look worried. Their friends must know what to do; this was their homeland after all. Then Michelle said, "There must be a crossing place somewhere, a raised sandbank where the water is shallow, but how do we find it?"

"I don't know," said Jean-Pierre, shaking his head. "But let's go down to the river, at least."

They pushed their ponies down the hill, letting them walk quietly now. The wild horses had slaked their burning thirst and were grazing peacefully close by. They lifted their heads as the children passed, but soon returned to their grazing.

At the water's edge, the children walked back and forth. Twice Jean-Pierre urged Folco into the river, but within a few steps the water was swirling round his knees and threatening to get deeper.

"There must be a way," said Jean-Pierre, half under his breath. "And we have got to find it." Just as he spoke, there was a soft whinny behind him. Looking round, he saw the stallion was calling his mares together and the little herd began to walk off. The children watched them, and almost as if he sensed he was not being followed now, the stallion stopped and turned.

"He's looking at us!" said Christopher. "You don't think he wants us to follow do you?"

"Sounds a bit far-fetched to me," said Jean-Pierre, a little grudgingly, "but let's follow them anyway!" The little herd trotted gently along by the water's edge, and then suddenly, the stallion turned sharply to the right. Without hesitating, he splashed into the water and the mares and foals followed him.

"It can't be deep there," cried Michelle, "he wouldn't take the foals into deep water."

The children watched. The little herd were half way across the river and still the water was no deeper than the foals' knees.

"Come on," said Jean-Pierre. "Quick before we lose the line. The sandbank will only be narrow."

In single file, they entered the water directly behind the wild horses. If they were nervous, they did not show it, although none of them spoke. All they could hear was the swishing of their ponies' legs and the splashing of their hooves as they gently ploughed through the water. Within minutes they were emerging on the other side.

"Phew," said Christopher. "I'm glad to be back on dry land." Susan look up to where the little band of wild horses were standing. The mares were grazing quietly again, the foals close by. The stallion was looking into the distance as if deciding where to take his little family next. Slowly he turned his head and looked for a long minute at the children. Then, with a low whinny to his mares, he was off again.

"He's so beautiful," Susan sighed. "Do you think he realised we did not know how to get across?"

"That's for you to decide," laughed Jean-Pierre. "But let's ride to the little house now. I'm sure it is Antoine's, and we can have a rest there before riding home."

Knowing they were safe now, the children began to talk about their adventure. Each one had his or her own tale to tell, their personal moment of glory that they felt to be the most important, but it was Susan who could cap them all.

"I bet," she said slowly, "I've been closer to a wild stallion than any of you!" As she spoke, she remembered, with a thrill of excitement, the flailing hooves, flaring nostrils and flying mane of her rescuer: the wild white stallion of the Camargue.

Wendy's War

by SUSANNAH BRADLEY

The station platform was crowded with children: big ones, small ones, fat ones, set of twins, brothers and sisters holding grimly on to each others' hands to make sure they did not get split up. Nearly all the little ones were crying. Even Wendy Turner, who at thirteen was one of the eldest, felt a lump in her throat when she thought of her mum in London where it was not safe.

There was a tug at her sleeve and she looked down to see seven-year-old Rosie Meadows from down her street looking at her pleadingly. "I want to spend a penny, Wendy."

Wendy looked along the platform to the long, long queue from the one convenience. Then she noticed a gap in the fence.

"Go on, there's bushes in there." Rosie took her hand, so Wendy followed her through the fence. "Look, there's flowers here. Let's pick some. We won't be missed."

She was wrong. By the time they got back through the fence, most of the children had been sent to the homes allocated to them. The Billeting Officer sighed when she saw them.

"Where have you two been?" she snapped. "You are lucky, Wendy, Mr and Mrs Brooks are still waiting, but Rosie will have to go to the Spinleys at West Gatehouse, The Hall. They weren't keen on taking an evacuee but that's too bad. There's a war on," and Rosie was bustled away.

Mr Brooks led Wendy over to a pony and trap in the lane, where his wife and daughter were waiting. They welcomed Wendy and she smiled as much as she could, but she could not help thinking of young Rosie, left on her own.

After a while, Mrs Brooks leaned forward and touched Wendy's arm. "There's our farm, down in that valley," she said.

Wendy looked, and there was a view she had only seen in glossy magazines in the dentist's waiting room. The little farm was set in green rolling hills, and the meadows were dotted with grazing animals. Wendy forgot about Rosie and feeling homesick. She was going to like it here.

As the weeks went by, Wendy felt she had never lived anywhere else. She fitted in with the farm life like a duck to water. Pam had her jobs and Wendy, after a couple of days, had hers. One of the jobs they shared was to search out the hens' eggs in nooks and crannies around the yard. It was a thrill to find more than three in one nest and an even bigger delight if they were still warm. There never seemed time to go looking for Rosie; there was so much else to do. Then, one day in July, Mr Brooks came in with a message for his wife.

"They want some of your strawberry tarts up at The Hall for a party. If you can do 'em I'll take 'em over on Saturday." It was agreed that Wendy could go too, to visit Rosie at the gatehouse.

Saturday was bleak and cold. Wendy wore some winter clothes that Pam had outgrown, and a pair of Wellington boots. The rain came down in sheets and the wheels of the cart threw up sprays of water from the puddles along the way.

"Now keep those gloves on," commanded Mr Brooks as he drove away from the gatehouse. Wendy nodded and turned to open the gate but a large angry dog leapt down the path and snarled at her. Wendy backed off.

"Don't go near him," said a voice behind her. "He's vicious." Wendy turned. Rosie stood there, but a very different Rosie. She had a sore on her mouth, matted hair, and was wearing a thin dress and battered plimsolls. Wendy stared at her.

"It's me, Wendy, don't you know me?" said Rosie.

"Yes," said Wendy slowly. "How are you?" As she said it she thought of the steaming plates of food at the farm and saw the hunger in her friend's eyes.

"Here," she said, fishing in her pocket. "I've got a pasty here, and some chocolate." Rosie snatched the offerings and crammed them in her mouth, all together. Then she fished a few squashed gooseberries out of her dress pocket.

"You can have these if you like. She doesn't know I took them." She jerked her head in the direction of the house, then cringed as a rough voice called her name. Rosie was gone in a flash, dodging past the dog to get indoors.

It was a good fifteen minutes before Mr Brooks returned to pick her up, and in that time Wendy could not stop thinking about Rosie. As soon as she was in the kitchen with Mr and Mrs Brooks she told them what was on her mind.

"She's a nice girl. She wouldn't be any trouble, and she looks as if she hasn't had a proper meal since she's been here." The Brooks looked at each other and shook their heads.

"We'd like to help, but you know we cannot afford to keep another child. Why don't you write to her mother?"

Wendy was disappointed, but decided to write the letter.

Dear Mrs Meadows,
Rosie is with some horrible people who don't look after her, so please come and take her back to London with you. Even if it's not safe it would be better than where she is now. Please hurry.   *Love, Wendy Turner*

Weeks went by, but there was no reply from Rosie's mother. After a month, Wendy wondered if she ought to write again. Then school broke up, and harvest time came, and everyone was so busy that Rosie went clean out of her head.

One day in early September, Pam and Wendy went on the Sunday School outing to Exeter. They sat together on the coach discussing how they would spend Wendy's egg money, and Pam's rabbit money. In Exeter, they could hardly wait for the tour of the cathedral to be over so that they could go to the shops.

"It's me, Wendy, don't you know me?" said Rosie

They never reached the shops, however. As they came out of the cathedral, Wendy noticed the slight figure of Rosie Meadows running past the entrance. She grasped Pam's hand and gave chase. They soon caught up with Rosie.

"Leave me alone, can't you?" cried Rosie. "I'm not going back there. You can't make me." The two girls hung on to her arms and looked at each other over her head.

"She'll have to go back," said Pam breathlessly.

"She won't," Wendy retorted. "Look what they've done to her. No wonder she's run away."

"I hid in a lorry this far," said Rosie. "I've been looking for signs to London, but there aren't any."

"Well, what can we do with her other than take her back?" asked Pam. "We can't let her go off on her own."

"All right, then—I'll go with her," said Wendy, suddenly. "I'm sorry about your mum and dad, Pam, they've been good to me. I suppose I should send the egg money back, but I'm going to need it." Pam reached in her pocket.

"You'll need more than that," she said. "Here, take my money too. Now get to the railway station quickly. I'll make some excuse for you." Wendy hugged her.

"Thanks, Pam," she said. Pam watched them run down the road, and whispered, "I do hope they get home."

Wendy and Rosie were soon at the station. Rosie marched towards the ticket office, but Wendy pulled her back.

"We don't want anyone to see us," she said quietly, "so I daren't buy tickets. We'll have to try to sneak on the train and then pay the ticket collector."

It was obvious that a train was due, as they could see through the slats in the high fence that the platform was lined with people. After walking the length of the fence without finding anywhere to sneak through, they made their way round by the road to the bridge that went over the track. They could see everything clearly. Wendy's heart began to beat faster.

"We've got to get down on that platform somehow. The indicator board says the next train's going to London."

"I can climb banks and things," said Rosie. "Look." She was through the railings in a flash, scrambling down the grassy bank which dropped steeply to the platform. Wendy had no choice but to clamber after her.

"Rosie! We'll be seen. It'll be awful!" They were not seen, for just as Rosie began her descent of the bank, the London train came steaming into the station and enveloped them in a cloud of yellowish-grey mist. In seconds they were on the train.

It was an awful journey. Wendy was terrified that they would be discovered and taken back. Rosie simply sat on someone's suitcase, happily sucking a lollipop that a soldier had given her, but even she started when, late that afternoon, there came the cry of, "Tickets please" from down the train. Wendy nudged Rosie and they made their way through to the next compartment's corridor where no one had seen them before.

"Copy me," she whispered, and she began to sniffle loudly. "Auntie Flo! Where are you?" she cried. Rosie joined in, and they were soon the centre of attention.

"Poor little mites. Lost, are you? Here, has anyone seen a woman looking for two kids? Anyone know Flo?" By the time the ticket collector arrived on the scene the whole compartment was in a state of uproar, calling out, "Auntie Flo" and tut-tutting about people who let children get lost on trains in wartime. Rosie and Wendy were given hot soup from flasks and sandwiches and sweets. The ticket collector asked a lot of questions.

"Ain't seen her since..." Wendy paused to think of a place they had passed through, "Taunton. Said she wanted something on the platform, and we never saw her again. She has got the tickets, too, though I've got some more money."

"And where was Auntie Flo taking you?" asked the man.

"Back home," piped up Rosie. She was not acting now, and her eyes filled with tears. "We were evacuated, see, but it was horrible. I missed my mum. I want my mum."

"We'll get you back to your mum, don't you fret," said the inspector, patting them on the head.

When they arrived at Paddington, he led them to the station-

The whole compartment was in a state of uproar

master's empty office, and told them to wait inside. Rosie sat down, but Wendy dragged her to a side door. Rosie objected.

"But Wendy, he's going to find our mums!"

"Use your loaf," said Wendy. "Our mums think we are in Devon. They'll send us back before we can explain."

"But it's getting dark," wailed Rosie. That could not be helped. They hopped on a bus which was going their way, and when they began to recognise the streets, they got off and walked on.

Suddenly the air was full of noise; a dreadful wail that made them shiver. They stood rooted to the spot, and around them people dived into shelters and pushed past each other in their hurry to get to safety.

"Come on, ducks, don't stand around when there's an air raid on," said a girl, pushing them ahead of her. Wendy and Rosie were hurried down some steps and carried along in a crush of people. Rosie gripped the edge of Wendy's coat and clung on tightly. Once or twice she stumbled.

"What's happening," she whispered. "Where are we?" As they were pushed round the next corner they saw a sign: Campden Town underground station. All around them, people were making themselves comfortable. There was very little space to lie down in the corridors of the tube station, but everyone was friendly and sympathetic when they realised that the girls were alone. They shared what food they had, and lent them some blankets. Both were soon asleep.

It was strange to wake the next morning and realise where they were. Around them, their friends of the night before slept on. A warden stopped them as they were leaving the station.

"Where's your gas masks, then?" he asked. They could not say, "In Devon" and Wendy could think of nothing to say. She looked down at her feet. Rosie began to cry.

"There, there, don't take on so," said the warden. "Left them at home, I expect? Well, don't forget again."

As they made their way through the sunlit streets, they could hardly believe their eyes. Entire streets were laid waste, a mass of rubble through which they had to pick their way. People were walking around aimlessly, crying and staring at the ruins of their old homes that had been bombed in the night. Soldiers were pulling down the walls that remained to make the ruins safe. Just a bit further, thought Wendy. Then it'll be all right. We'll be in our own street and Mum will be there. It never occurred to her that her own street might have been hit, so when they turned the corner they were unprepared for the devastation that met them. There was not a single house left standing.

"Where's Mum... and our house?" asked Rosie, clutching Wendy's skirt. Wendy could not answer her. She could only stare at the piece of sky which had once been blocked off by her own house, while she tried to bite back the tears.

They walked forward slowly. Wendy bent down at the edge of the rope which stopped the public from going too near the dangerous ruins. There, at her feet, was a photograph of her mother and herself, in the remnants of a frame.

"You live here, love?" A voice startled her from her daydream and she turned and saw an ARP warden.

"Yes," she said. "And she does too," nodding at Rosie.

"Where are your mothers? Did you get split up?" Wendy nodded. "I'm not surprised," rattled on the warden, "I've never known a night as bad as that. Now run along to the Baptist Church hall in Mere Street. They'll sort you out." He moved on.

"We'll have to," said Wendy to Rosie. "Even if they do find out we ran away, and they might not. Anyway, our mums could be there, and we don't have much choice." She took Rosie's hand and they walked towards the Baptist Church hall, gazing in astonishment at the terrible sights all around them. When they arrived at the hall, Rosie pulled her hand away.

"I'm not going in," she said. "They'll try to send me back." Wendy caught hold of her as she began to run, and managed to push the child inside the hall, tumbling in after her.

They stopped and looked round. It was even more chaotic than the underground station. The hall was packed with people, all milling around in an appalling jumble. Several officials were trying to take a roll call. Hungry children were crying.

A mass of rubble through which they had to pick their way

"Okay, you two, into the line, round this way," said someone, bustling them towards a trestle-table.

"Next. Names?" Wendy swallowed. She would have to risk it.

"Wendy Turner and Rosie Meadows," said she softly. The man ran his finger down the columns of his list. Wendy waited. His finger stopped, and he looked up at them inquiringly.

"Okay, you two. What's the game? You are supposed to be..." His words tailed off into silence as Rosie ducked her head and barged her way between the people, closely pursued by Wendy.

"Stop those two!" called the official, but no one could catch them as they forced their way to the door.

"I'm never going back," screamed Rosie as they reached the fresh air at last. She tore off down the street, tripped on a pile of rubble and fell on her face. Wendy caught up with her as she struggled to her feet. Rosie could feel the warm blood trickling down her leg as they ran on. Then suddenly there was a cry,

"Wendy, Wendy!" Wendy stopped and turned, pulling Rosie round with her. Then she began to walk back down the street, picking up pace until she was running and stumbling as fast as she could. In seconds she was in her mother's arms.

Much later, when all the explanations were over, Rosie, Wendy and her mother sat together in the Baptist Church hall with a hot cup of tea and a biscuit.

"Now that your mother is recovering from her emergency operation you can join her at your aunt's in Margate."

"I thought it was odd that she never replied to my letter," said Wendy. "It never occurred to me that she had never got it!"

"Will you go back to Devon now, Wendy?" asked her mother. Wendy thought about it for a moment.

"What about you, Mum?" she asked.

"I can't go anywhere. I've got a job in a munitions factory. I'm much too valuable!"

"Right then," said Wendy. "I'm not going anywhere either. We'll get somewhere to live. It was lovely in Devon, but I never felt I was really part of things until we got on that train to come back. I want to be here even if it is dangerous. It's my home."

A Time Gone By

by ANGUS ALLAN

"Sha hang fa wai ha'n cha'am." The shrunken oriental woman, sitting behind the stall of roots and powders, packeted potions and charms in the side alley off Nathan Road, Kowloon, leaned out and grasped Sally's arm in her bony claw. The ancient's bead-black eyes were sunk deep within the wrinkled face, like pinpoints seen through the wrong end of a pair of binoculars

"Come on, Sally," said her brother, Mike, tugging at her arm. "She's only another beggar." Sally's parents, Martin and Helen Chinnery, turned to hurry their daughter along.

"We haven't got all day, love. The bus for Kai Tak leaves in about ten minutes."

"She told me we mustn't catch our plane," said Sally.

Mr Chinnery laughed. "Suddenly, our Sally speaks Chinese! Ten days in Hong Kong, and she's jabbering the language! Do come on, Sal, and stop messing about."

"But, Dad! Honestly! I understood every word! There's danger…"

"Sally's been reading my comics," scoffed Mike. "She has looked on the whole place as mysterious and adventurous ever since we arrived."

"Well, I can't explain it," snapped Sally, stamping her foot. "As far as I know, the old woman spoke in English."

"Come on, it's about to go ..."

"Highly likely," said her brother, sarcastically, ignoring the fretting of their parents behind his shoulder. He waved his hand about, gesturing to the vivid banners hanging from every building, bright with Chinese ideograms that take even university scholars a whole lifetime to learn. "Apart from the tourists, the only people round here who speak our language are the tailors, and that's because they're from India and Pakistan. Even they're hard enough to talk to, because they all sound sort of Welsh, and jabber about 'being nice to come in and be having a suit made, in twenty-four hours, oh golly.'"

For once, Sally didn't bother to defend the Indians, whom she liked because of their smiling pleasantry. She was still insistent about the old pedlar woman. "I tell you it was a real warning!"

"Just behave youself, Sally." Her father was irritable now as the airport bus drew up. Typically, it had drawn across the heavy traffic of Nathan Road, to the sound of shrieking brakes and chattering insults from other drivers. "Hurry up and get in."

The bus had a drunken sign hanging on it, written in bad English, but it was clearly the bus that would take them to the airport at Kai Tak, where they were booked on the Mandarin Airways DC10 bound for their home in Sydney, Australia, via Manila in the Phillipines. Helen Chinnery clambered aboard as Martin hustled the baggage into the boot, but Sally, with Mike at her elbow, was looking back to where she had seen the old Chinese crone who had spoken to her. To her astonishment, neither woman nor stall were visible. Surely, they had been there—on the corner. Hadn't they? It couldn't have all been packed up and dismantled in a couple of minutes!

"Sal?" Mike was pulling at her sleeve now. "Come on, it's about to go..."

It could never have happened in Australia. Nor, perhaps, anywhere else where people wait and are patient. But in Hong Kong, bus drivers are not renowned for patience, and the doors hissed closed. Sally and Mike had a momentary impression of their mother and father, staring from the bus windows in dismay, and then the vehicle had gone, down past the Holiday

Inn and the Beefeater Bar, to turn left and disappear towards the Island Tunnel.

"Oh, crumbs. That's really done it!" Mike punched his sister on the shoulder. "They're going to be livid about this."

Sally grimaced. "I've got about twenty dollars of pocket money left. We'll get a taxi."

It was at that very moment that a cloud drifted over the sun. A deep, black cloud, with others clamouring behind it. In one second, as can only happen in that corner of the Far East, scorching heat gave way to the heavy promise of sudden, torrential rain. Sally and Mike ducked into the shelter of a doorway as the first drops fell. Above them, in the sky, there was a flaring burst of lightning, followed instantly by a shattering explosion of thunder. Sheets of water, as if poured suddenly by vindictive gods, cascaded about them, and shut off all but a metre of their vision. The heavens had opened.

There were no locals about. The Chinese know the city, and keep out of sight when such weather strikes, but had there been someone to observe, he would have seen the most incredible phenomenon. For as the children sheltered there, their bodies appeared to melt, and vanish away. In no more than twenty seconds, they had disappeared.

Mr and Mrs Chinnery were at Kai Tak airport. They were not happy. They had lost their children, and most of the officials at the place, being Chinese, were unable to understand their predicament. They had, however, managed to find a representative of Mandarin Airways, a fellow Australian, who had told them not to worry. "We've got problems with the flight, thanks to the bad weather. It'll be delayed. I'll get a call put out about Mike and Sally, and they'll be with you before take-off, I promise."

"I don't like it, Martin," said Mrs Chinnery. "What on earth can have happened to them? They aren't fools. They should have been here by now."

"Look, honey, you've got to calm down." Her husband took gentle hold of her hand, and his face was set and serious. "You're thinking of the past, aren't you?" he asked.

"How can I help it, Martin? It's like history repeating itself."

"Sally's father?" Martin Chinnery had dropped his voice to little more than a whisper. His wife nodded. "We've never told her that I was married before, or that Mike's only her half brother. Forgive me, Martin, but I can't help thinking about Dave."

Dave was Sally's real father. He was a pilot who had died, tragically, flying a Navy plane out of this very airport, Kai Tak, many years before. There had been a sudden squall. He had failed to correct. His aircraft had nosedived into the sea beyond the strip, and no trace of him had ever been found.

"Please, honey," said Martin Chinnery. "That's all in the past. Everything's going to be okay."

His wife stared at him. All she could think of was the strange warning that Sally had claimed to hear from the Chinese woman.

Meanwhile, the torrential rain beating around them, Sally and Mike were, as they thought, still sheltering in the Kowloon doorway. Constant glaces at her watch were making the girl more and more apprehensive, and her younger brother, four years her junior, jigged restlessly from foot to foot.

"We won't actually miss the plane home, will we?"

"Don't be silly, Mike. It'll still be there. Nothing can take off in this."

"Why not? They've got instruments and all sorts of things these days. I've read about them in books."

"Why don't you just shut up!" snapped Sally. "And don't start crying, for goodness sake! I couldn't bear it!"

To tell the truth, Sally wasn't far from tears herself. Neither Hong Kong Island nor the mainland beyond it is the sort of place to be marooned. She was frightened and felt totally alone. Then, almost in her ear, she heard a soft, lisping voice.

"Children. You come with me."

"Whaaat..?" Sally spun round, startled.

"Do not be afraid. I can help you." The words came slowly and were spoken with careful deliberation, but Sally was only aware that the wrinkled, kindly face of the old woman who had so suddenly appeared beside them was the same as that of the crone who had accosted her from the booth in Nathan Road. Mike knew it, too, by some extraordinary instinct he could not have explained. "She's talking in Chinese, but I can understand it..." he muttered.

"This way." The old woman beckoned, and reached out to produce a slim iron key, which she inserted into the door behind them—a door which they were sure was nothing but the portal of a disused shop, but now seemed to be that of an apartment building, solid and wooden and marked with strange Chinese characters.

"We oughtn't to follow", whispered Mike, thinking of all the things his parents had told him before the Hong Kong holiday; but he and his sister nevertheless followed the green-clad woman up the rickety stairs.

"Flight MA 360, Mandarin Airways to Sydney via Manila will depart in twenty minutes." The thin, crackling voice came over the Kai Tak speakers into the passenger lounge, where Mr and Mrs Chinnery were sitting with practically untouched coffee cups in front of them. "We're not going without them," said Mrs Chinnery, hysterically.

"Of course we're not. Look—everyone's doing what they can!"

Their airways contact hovered beside them. "We've got them," he said. "They are down at the police station and they're being brought here directly. They'll join you on the plane."

He was wrong. Two children had indeed been found wandering in the city, but thanks to the mix-up of languages, nobody knew that they were just ordinary Chinese orphans, loose in the big city. That was why, mistakenly lulled, Mr and Mrs Chinnery boarded the plane that was to take them away from Hong Kong, eagerly expecting Sally and Mike to be herded back to them before take-off.

The children, Sally and Mike, were in fact being ushered into

He and his sister followed the woman up the rickety stairs

a room of seedy appearance. Bamboo furniture was scattered about the place, and there was a bed made of woven rushes, upon which a young thin-faced European man lay, dressed in faded and stained khaki. He seemed aware of his half-naked chest as the children stopped in front of him, and he reached for a leather jacket to cover himself as he sat up.

"Sally?"

Sally peered at him. She felt no fear. She felt nothing except a strange, prickling sensation down her spine.

"I seem to recognise you," she said, then a second later added, "You look like me."

"I do at that," said the man. "Do you know Sydney, Australia?"

"I was born there."

Mike shifted his feet, nervously, and looked round at the impassive Chinese woman, who held his shoulder fast in her hand. "What is this?" he said.

"Sssh", she replied. "Let only your sister speak. She and the man."

"I'm no good." He sighed as he eased himself out of his bed. "I'm what you might call an adventurer, though some would call me worse. I married a nice lady, but I did my own thing and left her flat. She looked a lot like you..."

"I want to get back to my mother and father," said Sally, flatly. "Me and Mike here, we're lost. Can you see we get to Kai Tak airport, to find them?"

The man smiled. "I left her for a Chinese girl, but now I know better." He moved to Sally, and smoothed her hair. She felt the touch, but did not flinch. Instead, she looked around at Mike, and he was looking at her with his mouth agape.

"Come on, kids. I reckon we can make it. All of us." He nodded to the Chinese woman, who bowed back to him, and shrugged on his leather jacket as he shepherded Sally and Mike from the room.

Outside, in the street, a "champ" was waiting; one of those military vehicles that, as Mike said wonderingly, had been out of use for years. It took them straight to Kai Tak, where, through a wire-mesh gateway in the perimeter that the children had never seen before, Sally and her brother were taken by the man. He strode confidently across the tarmac towards an aircraft that stood ready and waiting to go: a twin engined aircraft with with Navy markings.

"Can we really go in this?" asked Mike, astonished. "It's not for civilians at all!"

"It's mine," said the man. "Up you go first, Sally." She hadn't even wondered how he knew her name.

In the cockpit, the man pressed earphones over his head, but said nothing. He made no contact with the control tower as he gunned the engines to full power, drifted out to the main runway, and took off, the rain falling around with undiminished violence. Sally gazed at him silently, still wondering that his face looked so familiar, so much like her own.

Flight MA 360 was in trouble. There had been an unpleasant incident in the passenger cabin on take-off. Two passengers, Mr and Mrs Chinnery, had been almost demented, screaming to be put off because their children had been left behind in Hong Kong. The stewardesses, though sympathetic, had to calm them down, telling them that the kids would undoubtedly be found and flown out on the next flight. The condition of weather was so bad that neither the captain nor the co-pilot had time to concern themselves with the customers. They had to fly this thing, this lumbering DC10, through the most awful storm, and that was that. Many a captain would not have taken off, but Donald "Daisy" Cutter was not about to let a rainbelt keep him from his schedule.

He was wrong in his judgement. He had hoped to climb far beyond the storm, to get into calm air, but he failed. The big plane shook and shuddered as it lifted through the clouds, and no sign came on in the cabins to tell the passengers to release their seat-belts. Violent slashes of lightning lanced down to surround the swaying machine, tonnes of deadweight in the hostile sky. One such blast from the heavens knocked out the entire

Its wings waggled twice, in some kind of signal

electronic guidance system of the plane, and left it in feeble human hands.

"If Geoff can find Manila, we're okay. Otherwise, we put down where we can see, Daisy," said the co-pilot.

Cutter snapped, "I'm dropping height. For pete's sake give me a fix, Geoff."

The navigator shrugged. With his equipment malfunctioning, he was as powerless as the others. "You tell me, Daisy."

Every member of the crew knew that the DC10 was likely to fall into the unfriendly Pacific, with disastrous consequences. Nobody would ever know what had happened to them. Pale stewardesses had to tell the passengers, and Mr and Mrs Chinnery clutched at each other, hopelessly. The plane continued to lose height.

"It's hopeless, Daisy! There's nothing but sea! We'll have to put her down into the waves!"

"I'll put her down when…" At that moment, Captain Cutter looked up. Another aircraft had shot beyond him, barely skimming him. Its wings waggled twice, in some kind of signal.

"We've got a guide," he yelled. "A Navy plane! See its registration! N-three five fifteen!"

Left and right, the big DC10 swung after its saviour. Then, through a split in the clouds, there was the sight of an island below. An airstrip! "It's Manila!"

Captain Cutter saw the Navy jet peel off. He set his flaps and spoilers, and came in for a perfect landing on an airport that had been entirely closed for traffic, thanks to weather conditions, for five hours. He knew he would be carpeted, would perhaps lose his licence, for daring to fly in the circumstances, but at least he knew his plane, his cargo of human beings, was safe.

Next day, at Darwin in the northernmost part of Australia, Mr and Mrs Chinnery disembarked from Flight MA 360 to be reunited with Sally and Mike. Neither of the children knew quite how they had come to be there, but there was no mistaking the joy of a family reunited.

"We were flown by a Navy jet," said Sally. "A nice pilot took us from Hong Kong, and brought us straight here. I slept a little on the flight, and so did Mike."

"But I dreamt," said Mike, "that we got in front of an airliner, and got it out of trouble. Maybe that's because I read too many comics."

"Where is this Navy pilot?" said their father.

Sally shrugged. "I don't know. He told us he couldn't stop around, and went away again. But he did say, and I thought it was funny, he did say give my love to Helen. How did he know that was your name, Mum?"

Mrs Chinnery swallowed hard. "I suppose you wouldn't remember anything about the pilot's plane, would you...?"

Sally said, brightly, "I know its number. It was N 3515."

Much later, when the family was back in Sydney, Helen Chinnery climbed to the attic of their home and picked out some papers from an old trunk. There was a telegram of sympathy from the Navy Board, with condolences from the Admiral for the death of her first husband, Sally's father. And there was a picture of the man beside the plane in which he had died. Clearly, on the fuselage, there was the marking—N 3515.

Today, neither Sally nor Mike believe in ghosts; but that is perhaps because their mother has never told them.

Beware the Northman!

by BRENDA RALPH LEWIS

It was a box, a small, roughly-made thing, or so it appeared to Christine until she scraped off some of the mud with her trowel.

"Good grief!" she breathed as she saw what was underneath. The first jewel that encrusted the lid of the box was deep blue. Even with mud smeared over it, it glowed up at Christine in the brilliant August sunshine. Carefully, using her thumb, she smoothed away more mud to reveal a red jewel, then a green one, both set in what looked to her like a lid made of gold. It was beautiful, stunning, a real treasure! Christine had no doubt about that. She sat back on her heels, gazing at her find with a feeling very much like awe. From what she could see of it, the box was covered in delicate decorations of scrolls and circles. Even the lock was beautiful: it was carved in the form of a minute rose.

Well, Christine thought with some satisfaction, this certainly makes up for not going to America with Mum and Dad. She had been very disappointed when her parents told her they could not afford to take her with them to New York to visit their married daughter Sue and her new baby. Next time, they had promised, but that was no comfort to Christine who had to spend the holidays with Mrs Ormerod, her mother's friend.

Mrs Ormerod herself was a nice woman, but her son John, at sixteen three years older than Christine, had made it clear from the start that he did not care to have "little girls" around the place. To make matters worse, Eyemouth, where the Ormerods lived, was a sleepy backwater, nothing like the exciting, dynamic place Christine imagined New York to be. As if that were not enough to make a thorough ruin of this year's summer holidays, Christine had to spend the daytime in the same place as the taciturn John—on the site of the old Anglo-Saxon village near Eyemouth which John was helping to excavate. There was no help for it, though, not with Mrs Ormerod out at work all day.

Of course, there was a bit of drama about the site, for eleven centuries ago it had been attacked and destroyed by Viking raiders, and all the inhabitants had either been killed or taken off as slaves. There was even a rumour that the site was haunted. Two small children had been seen, apparently searching for something. No one knew who they were. They did not come from Eyemouth, as far as anyone could tell, but none of the local folk who had seen them had ever dared to go close enough to find out. You did not meddle with ghosts, and that's what local legend believed these youngsters to be.

The idea that there were ghosts around, though Christine only half believed it, made it even less tempting for her to spend six whole weeks mucking around in the mud of the village site. John Ormerod had, of course, been furious at the thought of Christine tagging along. He had made his opinion very clear, too. Every morning for a whole week now, he had stalked out of the house with a frown on his face, and he and Christine had made their way to the excavations in complete silence.

When they got there, Brian King, the leader of the dig, usually sent Christine to some far corner of the site, well away from John and the wattle-and-daub hut he was working on at the perimeter of village. Christine was not exactly sorry about that, but it did make her feel an unwanted nuisance. That feeling persisted after she and John got home when the day's work on the site was over. John's morose manners made for long, uncomfortable silences at dinner. It was extremely embarrassing, too, when he got up from the table without a word after the meal was over and disappeared to his own room for the evening.

Had it not been for the fact that Christine chummed up with Marjorie Rawlings, a cheery, warm-hearted girl who was helping out at the excavations, she would have felt a thorough outcast. Marjorie had been furious when Christine told her of John and his bad moods.

"Why don't you speak to his mother?" Marjorie had suggested angrily. "Surely she can make him behave properly?"

Christine shook her head. "I think Mrs Ormerod's afraid of John," she said. "She's sort of nervous all the time, as if she expects something awful to happen at any moment."

Marjorie would have none of that. "Well, I know what I'd do! That John needs a good hiding! It would give me great pleasure to give him a thump or two. Who on earth does he think he is, acting all superior like this?"

Christine could not help being amused. She had no doubt that Marjorie Rawlings would have given John a very good hiding, and made sure it hurt. Marjorie was one of those large, strong country girls who stood no nonsense from anyone. Besides, she had three brothers. Growing up in their company, it was no wonder that boys held no terrors for Marjorie.

Now, though, with the little box nestling in the palm of her hand, John Ormerod and the uncomfortable atmosphere he created, faded from Christine's mind. Now, she knew what people meant when they said that archaeology was "history in your hand", and that it could bring the most thrilling of experiences.

Marjorie was working a few metres away, searching out the ring of depressions in the earth which marked where the old Anglo-Saxons had once built a defensive stake-fence. Christine called her over, and Marjorie whistled appreciatively as she saw the box.

"Is it valuable, do you think?" Christine asked, very much hoping that it was.

Marjorie pursed her lips. "I don't know—only Brian King could tell that for sure. If you could get more of the mud off, though, we might get a slightly better idea!"

After a few minutes in the warm August sunshine, the mud had dried off a little, and Christine was able to flick some of it away with a fingernail. As she did so, she saw several marks carved on the box which did not seem to be part of the overall pattern. Marjorie peered at them. "Look like runes to me!" she said authoritatively.

"Runes? What are they?"

"A sort of alphabet—the Anglo-Saxons used it, so did the Germans, and the Vikings, too! The Vikings thought there was magic in the runes, as a matter of fact!"

Christine felt rather excited. Perhaps the runes formed some sort of magic message. It was just as she was looking more closely at the rune marks that she became aware of the dents and scratches on the box. It had suffered some rough handling at some time. Maybe it had been crushed underfoot during that Viking raid long ago. Christine shuddered as she thought of it. She felt sad all of a sudden, and not for the first time, either. More than once since she first came to the village site, Christine had sensed the presence of the marauding Vikings all round her. They were the ghosts here, as far as she was concerned, not those two mysterious children of local legend. Some people said that violence and destruction left their mark on time, and that a place where these things had occurred always carried a sort of invisible image of them. Perhaps it was so here. Christine could not help picturing the terror that had once pervaded this place. It must have been horrible—the murderous Vikings rampaging through the village brandishing their swords, the flames, the screams, the villagers running wildly, desperately trying to escape into the surrounding forest.

The hillside where the village had once stood was now a lush stretch of green grass. The forest of Anglo-Saxon times was gone. The summer sky was bright above and it was all so beautiful and peaceful now. It hardly seemed possible that this had once been the scene of so much suffering and fear.

"What's the matter, Chris?" It was Marjorie, jerking her back to reality. "You're looking glum all of a sudden!"

Christine could not help picturing the terror

Christine looked up, abashed at being caught daydreaming. "It's nothing—just thinking!" she said. Here, look at this!"

It happened just as Christine traced a fingertip around the rose-shaped lock to draw Marjorie's attention to it. A wind. A cold blast of air from nowhere that made her shiver. It was weird.

"Chris, are you all right?" It was Marjorie again, this time sounding quite concerned.

Christine looked hard at her. "Didn't you feel it?" she asked.

"Feel? What?"

"Something ... a cold wind blowing..." Christine was suddenly aware of how ridiculous it sounded.

"What are you talking about? It's sweltering out here!" Christine felt scared, and to cover up the feeling, gave a small smile.

"Must be my imagination!" she shrugged. Of course it was her imagination. The whole site was basking in glorious sunshine, with not a breeze to stir the bushes or ruffle the trees.

Christine was just dismissing the whole episode when it happened again. This time, she actually felt the wind lift her air off her shoulders for a brief moment; and it was colder than before. Christine glanced quickly at Marjorie, but without even asking, she could see that Marjorie was totally unaware of anything peculiar. Something very strange was going on, Christine was sure, but what? Once she could have imagined a cold wind on a blazing hot day, but not twice. It was this place, Christine decided, this old village with the atmosphere of long-ago violence still hovering over it.

Marjorie had been scrutinising Christine, and did not like what she saw.

"Look here, my girl!" she was saying in that hearty way of hers. "You're looking quite green round the gills. This heat's getting at you—come on, what you need is a bit of shade and a glass of water!" Marjorie put out a large hand and pulled Christine to her feet. "Come on, Chris!" she said firmly. "You want to show Brian what you've found, don't you?"

Marjorie was being motherly and a bit patronising. Though

only two years older than Christine, she got into this mood sometimes. Christine imagined it was due to all the practice she got mothering those brothers of hers. Christine had met two of them, the twins Graham and Peter. They were tall and strongly built even at fourteen, and it was no surprise to Christine when they told her they were keen rugby players at school. The third brother, Tom, was much older. He worked odd hours, which was why Christine had not met him. All three adored Marjorie and would do anything for her, so there was no doubt who was the dominant one in the family. Now that Marjorie had taken charge of this situation, Christine had no mind to resist.

"Yes, you're right!" she told Marjorie as brightly as she could. Christine looked across the site and spotted Brian King working not far from the wattle-and-daub hut, cleaning some pottery which had been found yesterday. "Let's take it to him now!"

All at once, just as Christine was starting off in Brian's direction, with Marjorie close behind, she heard the voice. It was a young child's voice, whispering to her, as if from far, far away.

"No... no! Take it to Eostre! Please, the Northman must not have it. Take it to Eostre!" The last word faded off into silence like a sigh. Christine had halted in her tracks, heart pounding. She was aware that she had turned very pale. This was not just a touch of the sun, whatever Marjorie said. Christine looked at her companion. Marjorie must have heard the voice. It was so clear, or at least it had been clear to Christine, but Marjorie's answering gaze was quizzical. She had heard nothing.

When they reached Brian King, it was Marjorie who, characteristically, did all the talking. Christine was glad. She was still feeling rather shaken after the strange experiences she had had and wanted more than anything to get away and have a good think. She got little chance to mull things over in the enthusiasm that arose when the other helpers on the site came crowding round to have a look at her "find".

"Well done, young Chris!" Brian King congratulated her. "This looks a pretty important discovery to me!" Brian perused the box appreciatively. The strange winds and even the faraway

Christine was less pleased when Brian called John over

voice faded to the back of Christine's mind as she basked in the praise.

She liked Brian King, and felt very flattered by his words. She regarded him as a sort of elder brother, the kind young sisters look up to. Though he was probably around thirty years old, he looked a lot younger and seemed to get on well with the youngsters helping out on the village site.

Christine was less pleased, though, when Brian called John Ormerod over to have a look at the box. The unsociable John had stayed by the hut he was excavating when everyone else had downed tools to crowd round Brian. John came over, reluctantly, scowling at being interrupted.

"Typical!" Christine heard Marjorie mutter as she saw John's sour expression.

"This young lady of yours has done us a favour, eh, John?" Brian said breezily, handing him the box. Brian glanced at Christine and gave her a big wink. She smiled at the spectacle of John being teased.

John's answer was predictable. "She's not my young lady!" he muttered. He glowered at Brian, who grinned broadly at him. "Yes," John agreed, rather grudgingly. "It's quite a good find!" He handed the box back to Brian.

"More than quite a good find!" Brian retorted, tracing his fingers over the jewels embedded in the top of the lid. Christine, watching, had the feeling there was something almost greedy about Brian's gesture, but she dismissed the thought at once. Her imagination had done quite enough overtime for one day.

"Is it worth something, then?" Christine asked eagerly.

Brian gave her a smile. "Oh, yes, I should think so—worth more than you might imagine, maybe!"

Suddenly, Christine saw John Ormerod looking at Brian rather sharply, as if he was alarmed by something Brian had said. Brian saw it too.

"What's the matter now, John? I'm not giving away any state secrets, you know!" Brian turned to Christine and explained, "When our sponsors at the Lady of Easter Museum see this find

143

of yours, they'll be impressed, I can tell you! It's just the sort of thing we need to convince them that their money is well invested in this whole dig." Brian laughed. "Much better than a lot of broken old pots, to be sure. Old pots don't look nearly so good on display—we've got to think of things like that, you know! You can be very proud of yourself, young lady!"

"Brian!" It was John, calling across to him in a strange, tight voice. He sounded worried about something. "Er... come over here to the hut will you? There's something I want you to see!"

Brian gave Christine a parting grin. He leaned towards her and whispered, "Wonder what young grizzleguts has got up his sleeve?" Christine could not help being amused. "Young grizzleguts" was a very good name for John Ormerod.

That evening, when work on the site was over, John seemed to be in a worse temper than ever. He marched off in the direction of home without a word to Christine, and she had quite a job catching up with him. John had quarrelled with Brian after he called him over to the hut. No one had heard what they said to each other, but everyone was sure they had exchanged some pretty hot words, and not only because of the way John was behaving, either. Brian, too, had that tight-faced, tight-lipped look which betrayed anger only just below the surface, and he too, stalked off the site without saying goodnight to anyone.

Brian did not even bother to make sure that the pottery table was cleared, and the finds properly put away. It was very unusual for him. The youngsters who had been helping with the cleaning were all at sea without Brian to tell them what to do. Fortunately, though, capable Marjorie took over and organised them, and the tidying up was done before it got dark.

Hopefully, whatever John and Brian had argued about, it would all blow over by tomorrow. Otherwise, the atmosphere on the site would be intolerably tense.

Christine found the incident very frustrating, for it robbed her of the chance to discuss with Marjorie all the strange things that had occurred after she found the little box. At first, Christine had been afraid to mention anything so fanciful in case

John seemed to be in a worse temper than ever

down-to-earth Marjorie thought her a ninny with an overheated imagination, but the more Christine thought about it, the more she was convinced that she had heard something, and that she was faced with a mystery she simply had to unravel.

Who or what was Eostre? Christine had never heard the name before, and why was there such fear and pleading in the faraway voice in case "the Northman" got hold of the little box? "Northman" was another name for Viking, Christine knew that much, but there were no Vikings at the site or anywhere. The Vikings had ceased to exist as a separate people centuries ago.

It was all too much for Christine to keep to herself. Marjorie might know the answers, she thought hopefully. Marjorie was brainier than her appearance suggested. She look like one of those rosy-cheeked large-made country girls, who grew up to work on a farm and milk cows. In actual fact, Marjorie wanted to be an archaeologist when she grew up, and she already knew quite a bit about the subject and about the Vikings and Anglo-Saxons who had once inhabited this part of northern England.

Now, however, without Marjorie to talk to, Christine felt doubly curious and impatient to find the answers to the un-answered questions that were revolving in her mind. As she walked back to Mrs Ormerod's house, the queries kept nagging at her, tantilising and mysterious. Christine watched John pacing quickly ahead of her, and it crossed her mind that maybe she could ask him for a few explanations, but she dismissed that idea almost immediately. The way John Ormerod was walking, in quick, angry strides, his shoulders hunched, he was not in the mood to be asked anything. The argument with Brian must have been very serious, Christine decided. Best leave John alone and best not to mention finding that little box on the site, either. Christine was bursting to tell Mrs Ormerod of her excit-ing discovery, but she sensed that John would not like it.

Just then, a thought struck her. "Take it to Eostre!" the far-away voice had pleaded. Eostre... a strange sounding name, not like a person's name at all. A place, maybe?

"Yes, why not?" Christine mused. "Maybe it's near here?" She

146

glanced out over the majestic sweep of landscape around her, the hills studded with rocky outcrops and the fresh smell of the River Tweed as it plunged down towards the smooth sands of the North Sea coast. Just the sort of place to tuck away a tiny village with an odd name. The place names of Northumberland had always struck Christine as strange, not at all like the ones she was accustomed to down south, near London where she lived. Maybe Eostre was a tiny place hidden in the fold of a hill, with a few houses, a general store, perhaps a post office, but not much more. The sort of place no one would bother to put on a map, and only local people would know much about—people like Mrs Ormerod. Perhaps she would know where Eostre was.

When Christine reached the house, though, she found Mrs Ormerod was too busy making dinner, and the chance to ask her did not arise until they were all sitting down to their meal. To Christine's disappointment, Mrs Ormerod looked blank when she heard the name.

"Eostre? No, there's nowhere round here with a name like that, dear!" she said. "Eostre..." Mrs Ormerod mulled it over, but finally shook her head. "Sorry, Christine dear, I can't help."

Back to square one, Christine thought. Her guess had obviously been wrong. With a jolt, she realised that John was looking at her very piercingly from across the table. His eyes were like magnets and she could not help looking back at him.

"Why do you want to know about Eostre?" he snapped at her.

"John, don't be so rude!" cried Mrs Ormerod.

John ignored her. "Why are you asking about Eostre?" he repeated grimly. Christine felt terrible. An innocent, even inocuous question, was turning into something very much like an interrogation. She wished she had never mentioned the subject.

Christine was tongue-tied for a moment, but managed to blurt out, "I...I heard the name. I just wondered what... I mean, where... it was."

She felt herself going red as she spoke, and out of the corner of her eye saw Mrs Ormerod looking very upset. She was trying to hide it by fiddling with the cutlery. All at once, Christine felt very angry. Marjorie's words about John came back to her, and Christine thought how right she had been. Who on earth did John Ormerod think he was, acting in this superior fashion?

"I only asked a simple question!" Christine burst out suddenly. "There's no need to make a big thing out of it!"

John, she could see, was taken aback by her outburst. Till now, Christine had been somewhat quiet, even a bit timid, if only because she did not want to make life more difficult for Mrs Ormerod. Now, though, she had found her voice and it was a furious one. Now it was Christine who was glaring across at John, daring him to say one rude word more.

It was quite a transformation, and beneath her anger, Christine experienced a certain pleasure at seeing John quail beneath her gaze. Serve him right—it was about time he got some of his own medicine.

"Well, you heard what Mum said..." John mumbled, looking very disconcerted. "We've never heard of Eostre!"

John got up from his seat, threw down his napkin and walked quickly from the room. It looked to Christine as if he could not get out fast enough. She heard him run up the stairs two at a time, and then the door of his room slammed shut.

In the silence that followed, Christine realised that Mrs Ormerod had started to cry.

"I'm sorry, Mrs Ormerod," she said awkwardly. "I didn't know John was going to get so upset." Mrs Ormerod reached out a hand, and Christine took it in hers, hoping to comfort the unfortunate woman. It was all her fault. She should never have said anything about Eostre. If only she had not been so impatient. She should have waited until the morning and asked Marjorie.

"You're ... you're not to blame, dear!" Mrs Ormerod said softly, reaching for her handkerchief and wiping her eyes. "Please don't feel bad about it. I don't know what's the matter with that boy. He was always a bit difficult, you know... moody, especially since his father died; but it's got much worse recently."

"Recently? What do you mean?" Mrs Ormerod looked at Christine, her eyes red-rimmed. She was very distressed.

"You're ... you're not to blame, dear!" Mrs Ormerod said softly

"It's that old village site," she whispered. "It's as if it has cast a spell on him, like an obsession." Unable to stop herself, Mrs Ormerod began to cry again. After a few moments, though, she managed to go on. "He doesn't think about anything else. He spends all his time poring over those old, dusty books of his. I don't know what to do about it, honestly I don't!"

Christine was intrigued. "What books, Mrs Ormerod?" she asked.

"Oh, just old books about history—local history I think," Mrs Ormerod replied. "You know, about the old Anglo-Saxons and Vikings. It wasn't too bad, I suppose, until John found that box at the excavations."

Christine gasped. "What box?" She knew her voice sounded sharp with surprise, but she could not help it. "Please tell me about it, Mrs Ormerod," she went on, more quietly.

Christine need not really have asked. She already knew what Mrs Ormerod was going to say. The box John had found was the exact replica of hers, jewel encrusted lid, rose shaped lock, rune marks and all. It seemed, though, that the box had got Mrs Ormerod into a certain amount of trouble, for quite clearly she had not been meant to know about it.

"It was one evening when John was out," Mrs Ormerod explained, her voice trembling. "He went over to see Brian King, to discuss something about the excavations, I suppose. I went up to John's room to tidy it up, and while I was there, I found the box in one of the cupboards." Mrs Ormerod sighed. "But then, John came back unexpectedly. He'd forgotten something, I suppose and he was very angry when he saw me with the box in my hand. Oh, dear…" Mrs Ormerod's voice broke as if she was going to start crying again. She turned to Christine, with an anxious look. "I really shouldn't be telling you all this. Please don't let John know I told you."

"No, of course I won't!" Christine promised. She was feeling extremely sorry for Mrs Ormerod and angrier than ever with John for causing her so much distress.

Mrs Ormerod blew her nose. "Oh my, what a carry on!" she

said. She was making great efforts to cheer herself up and managed a wan smile. "I suppose that this is what happens when you're dealing with one of those furious Vikings!"

"What? You mean John...John's a Viking?" Christine cried. "A Northman?"

"Well no, not exactly," Mrs Ormerod told her. "There aren't any Vikings any more, are there? But the Ormes and Ormerods were certainly Vikings years and years ago..." Mrs Ormerod stopped, noticing the startled look on Christine's face. "What's so surprising about it, dear? Is it important?"

Christine could only stare at her, round-eyed with astonishment. All she could think of was the voice she had heard on the village site, whispering to her out of the air. "The Northman must not have it!" it had pleaded. Could it have meant John?

That night, Christine found it impossible to get to sleep. For four or five hours, maybe more, she tossed and turned, but eventually chose to get up and sit by the window. There, she hoped, the cool night air might clear her mind and enable her to work out some meaning to the strange events of the previous day.

So, two boxes had been found on the site of the old Anglo-Saxon village! Then why had Brian not mentioned there were two? That seemed odd for a start; and why should John have made such a fuss when Mrs Ormerod found the other box, the one he had unearthed? Was there any significance in John's Viking ancestry, or was it just a coincidence? Christine could understand that it would increase John's interest in excavating a village which the Vikings had once raided, but she had an odd idea that there was something more to it than that.

Christine was getting sleepy now, at last. Her eyelids were becoming heavy and she found her head kept dropping forward. She was dimly aware that a wind had sprung up outside, a cool, fresh wind that rustled the leaves of the big oak tree in one corner of the garden. Except that it was not the leaves rustling.

"Please help us...please..." Christine jerked abruptly awake. She looked quickly round in the garden, but it was full of dark impenetrable shadows, nothing else.

Two small children seemed to be standing beneath the oak tree

"Please..." the voice sighed at her. "We tried to get to Eostre, but we could not. The Northmen prevented us..."

Christine's drowsiness had vanished and she was totally alert now. She peered into the garden again, scrutinising the shadows more carefully. Slowly, as she watched, one of the shadows took form. Two small children seemed to be standing beneath the oak tree. One seemed quite small, perhaps only about four or five years old. The other, holding the little mite's hand, was taller and seemed to be looking straight at Christine.

"The Northman is coming. Please help. He must not have the treasure, it belongs to Eostre ... Eostre..." As the voice wafted into Christine's ears, the outline of the two children began to grow fainter before her eyes. She looked hard at them, trying to imprint their images on her mind. Long, shaggy hair, roughly made tunics rather like sacking, bare feet—just like the Anglo-Saxons used to dress long, long ago. No wonder no one in Eyemouth knew who these children were, Christine thought with a twist of fear inside. No wonder she had felt a cold wind on the site yesterday afternoon as they hovered around her.

"Ghosts," Christine whispered to herself. "There are always cold winds when ghosts are around. Heavens, I'm seeing ghosts."

The two children were fading fast, and the voice was so faint now that she could not hear any distinct words. Christine was suddenly filled with anxiety. She had to get out into the garden and speak to them, she had to know more. "No, wait ... don't go!" Quickly, Christine turned away from the window. In seconds she was at the door, pulling it open, then out on to the upstairs landing where, all of a sudden, she stopped short.

There was only a faint shaft of light to see by, but it was enough for Christine to see down the stairs into the hall below. There was someone there. Christine pressed back against the wall, her heart beating very fast. She risked leaning forward a little to take another look. Whoever it was seemed to be huddled against the wall, hunched over as if he had something to hide.

"Yes, I know it's the middle of the night!" John Ormerod's voice was only a quiet mutter, but Christine heard it clearly in the deep silence of the night. "Use your head! How could I phone you with Mother around—or that wretched little girl?"

Christine bristled. John was referring to her, but what was he doing making a telephone call at this hour? It must be two, maybe three in the morning.

"What do you mean, you haven't done it yet?" John was saying in an urgent whisper. "Why not? I thought you were supposed to be the expert on runes. Can't you get any sense out of them?"

Christine heard John give a sharp sigh of impatience. "It's no use saying you need more time!" he snapped. "We haven't got any more time! It's that girl, Christine. She's been asking about Eostre. She thought it was a village round here! Imagine that!" John gave a dry, tense laugh. "But she's not as innocent as she looks, that one—she'll soon find out Eostre was a Saxon goddess—and remember she was the one who unearthed that second box, so Lord knows what else she's discovered—or guessed!"

Then there was a long pause. The person at the other end of the line was trying to assure John that he was worrying about nothing, or so Christine imagined. John was very worried, however, Christine was certain. His voice was tense and tight.

John stopped the flow of words from the other end of the line with an abrupt, "It's all your fault, Brian!" Brian! Christine prickled all over as she heard the name.

"Yes, it's your fault, so don't deny it!" John went on. "If you hadn't been so cocky and confident at the site this afternoon, that wretched girl would never have become so curious!" John was wrong about that, Christine reflected. Brian's behaviour this afternoon had not made her specially curious, but John's behaviour now was certainly doing so.

"You should have let her think the box was just another find—not something special! No, I'm not being over anxious ... the girl knows something, maybe quite a lot. Don't give me any more of your smooth talk, Brian King!" The irritation was growing in John's voice. "You solve those runes by tomorrow, or else I'm pulling out of this whole business... Yes, I do mean it! We've got to start digging, and in the right place, tomorrow night... Yes, that's what I said. No, I haven't found any clues in those old books you gave me... I've read them till my eyes have practically dropped out. Whoever wrote them wasn't giving anything away! Only the runes on those boxes will tell us where to look. You've got them both now, so get on with it! I don't care if you are up all night, either! All right, then—goodbye!"

Quickly, as John put the receiver down, Christine drew back into the shadows of the upstairs landing. She had been practically transfixed by what she had heard, so much so that John was half way up the stairs before she realised it. As quickly and quietly as she could, Christine slipped back into her room and pushed the door to. She heard John pass by, and risked a quick glance through the chink in the door. If John Ormerod had been looking worried before, he seemed frantic now. Christine saw him biting his lip with anxiety, and he had wrapped his arms about himself as if to find protection from some danger.

"Wow!" Christine murmured to herself. There was more to this than she had at first thought. Whatever plot Brian and John were mixed up in, it must be something pretty serious, maybe, Christine hesitated at the thought, maybe even criminal. No wonder John had been so unwelcoming when she came to stay with his mother at Eyemouth. The last thing a plotter wanted was a curious intruder on the premises.

However, Christine was much more than merely curious or intrigued now. Unwillingly, she had become involved in the nefarious doings of Brian King and John Ormerod. It was not just what John's furtive middle of the night telephone call had told her—that "her" box, the second one, completed some sort of secret message which the two conspirators had been waiting for. No, it was those two pathetic little wraiths who were uppermost in Christine's mind now. Sitting in the silence of her room, with the cool of the night all round her, Christine remembered the desperate note in the voice of the ghost-child. One glance out of the window had told her that the two children were gone now, but their restless spirits were still about. She could feel they were there. Christine pictured the two children wandering across the centuries that lay between their time and her own, troubled by some task they had left undone, and urgently seeking for someone, anyone, who could help them.

Why they should have chosen to communicate with her, Christine could not imagine, but what she did know was that she could not ignore their appeal. For unless she succeeded, somehow, in completing their task for them, those poor little spirits might wander through time for ever.

To her surprise, Christine felt quite fresh and alert when she woke next morning, even though she could not have had more than three or four hours' sleep. It was the sound of the front door closing and the crunch of footsteps on the path that woke her up. It must be John, leaving without her. It was far too early for Mrs Ormerod to be going to work just yet—only eight o'clock, in fact. Christine leaped out of bed and ran to the window just in time to see John walking away along the road that ran beside the garden hedge. He must be making for the village site to have a word with Brian before any of the others arrived.

There was no time to waste. Christine managed to get washed and dressed in four minutes flat, and hurtled downstairs to bolt down her breakfast in record time. Before the startled Mrs Ormerod could ask her what all the rush was about, she was pelting along the road towards the excavations.

When she got there, she found John and Brian deep in whispered conversation, standing in a spot well away from Marjorie Rawlings and the one or two other workers who had also arrived by this time. Christine made herself walk casually over to Marjorie. She wanted to run, but that would only have made John suspicious, and that was the last thing Christine wanted.

"What are they talking about? Do you know?" Christine whispered urgently to her friend, glancing over at Brian and John.

Marjorie disentangled her arm. "What's up, Chris? You look all flustered!"

"What are they talking about?" Christine's voice was very insistent now and startled Marjorie.

"What's up, Chris? You look all flustered!"

Marjorie shrugged. "How do I know? I haven't go bionic ears! They seem to have made up their quarrel, though, and they're agreeing about something. There's been a lot of nodding going on! That's all I can say. Now will you tell me what this is all about?"

Keeping her voice low, Christine told Marjorie everything. Marjorie listened, her eyes widening with each revelation. "Great Scott. You've certainly stumbled on something!" she breathed in amazement. "But those children—are you sure?"

"Of course I am! I didn't imagine it, Marjorie, I know I didn't!"

Marjorie surveyed Christine's face and saw the look of total conviction stamped on it. "No, I don't think you did imagine it, Chris," she said quietly. "I knew the stories about those children haunting this old village site, but I thought they were just superstitious tommy-rot!"

"And now?" Christine queried.

"If you've seen and heard them, that's good enough for me," Marjorie assured her. "And from what you've told me, it seems that the rest of the legend might be true!" Now, it was Christine's turn to look surprised.

"The rest of legend?"

"Oh yes, there was more to it than just a couple of ghosts spooking about the place!" Marjorie told her. "When the Vikings raided the village, those two kids are supposed to have fled towards the village church for protection, but they were killed on the way."

"Oh, gosh, how terrible!" There were tears in Christine's eyes as she thought of it.

"But that's not all," Marjorie said. "The children had been given something by their father, something important, to hide in the church so that the Vikings wouldn't find it!"

"The box—it must have been the box I found yesterday!" Christine said excitedly.

"Yes, I think it was. But it wasn't just the box itself that was important, it must have been the secret it contained, or rather the half of the secret it contained..." Marjorie broke off.

"Chris! I think I've got it!" she exclaimed, a bit too loudly for Christine's liking. She looked round, but no one was near.

"Try this for size, Chris!" Marjorie was saying. By the look on her face, she was in the grip of some intriguing theory. "We know from what John said to Brian on the 'phone last night that there's some sort of message, or maybe directions, to some treasure carved on the two boxes. But one box is not enough. To read the message in the runes, you have to have both of them. Follow me so far?"

"Yes, yes, go on!" Christine found Marjorie's excitement catching.

"The first box, the one Mrs Ormerod told you John found, was already in the village church at the time of the Viking raid," Marjorie went on, warming to her theme. "The children were taking the other box, the one you found, to put with it..."

"But that's ridiculous!" Christine interrupted. "Surely, if the villagers wanted to keep the secret of the boxes, they would have kept them in separate places. Otherwise the Vikings might have found both boxes and discovered the secret."

Marjorie smiled. "Top marks for logic, Chris, but remember, eleven centuries ago, people didn't think logically about such things. They thought a church was a sanctuary, holy ground, the safest place on earth, where nothing could harm them—or their secret!"

"But the voice kept telling me 'Take it to Eostre', not 'Take it to the church!'" Christine protested.

"Same thing!" Marjorie replied promptly. "You see, when the Anglo-Saxons became Christians, they didn't give up all their old gods and goddesses. They sort of took their goddess Eostre and some of the others to church with them! They had a festival called Guil—that's where the Yule log at Christmas comes from—and the goddess Eostre gave her name to Easter!"

"So she became ... well, the Lady of Easter, I suppose," Christine murmured. "Like the museum that's sponsoring this dig."

"Exactly—and the church near it. That's its name: the Church of Our Lady of Easter!" Marjorie told her.

"Tom will be along later," Marjorie assured Christine

So that was it, Christine thought. That's what the ghost voice had been talking about: it wanted her to take the little box, or the treasure, or both to the church at Eyemouth! Then, Christine gave a rueful sigh.

"This is all very well, but it doesn't help us to deal with Brian and John, does it?" she told Marjorie. "Oh, Marje," she went on, a break in her voice. "We've just got to stop them getting hold of that treasure, if only for the sake of those children."

"There's only one thing we can do!" said Marjorie. Her voice had that capable mothering tone again. "We've got to be here when those two start digging tonight. That clump of bushes over there." Marjorie nodded towards the bushes, which lay just outside the perimeter of the village, where the hill sloped downwards in a smooth incline. "We can hide there and watch them!" To Christine the very idea sounded crazy.

"But what can we do?" she protested. "A couple of girls—John and Brian are much stronger than we are!"

"Speak for yourself, young Chris!" said Marjorie loftily. "I've promised myself that John Ormerod is going to get a good hiding and he jolly well is! You just leave it all to me!"

Christine lay, front down, on the hill slope behind the bushes, digging her toes into the earth in case she slid from her position. Marjorie had managed things better. She had found a tree root embedded in the ground on which to balance herself. Next to her, crouched two of her three brothers, the twins Graham and Peter. The third brother, Tom Rawlings, must be working those odd hours of his again, or so Christine presumed.

"It's all right," Marjorie assured Christine. "Tom will be along later. It's all arranged."

In the meantime, though, Peter and Graham did very well as the reinforcements Marjorie had promised to bring with her. If it came to using fists, Christine reflected, John and Brian were going to have a hard time handling those two, and Marjorie herself, Christine imagined, was no mean hand at throwing punches, either.

As the day had worn on, it became plain that John and Brian

were itching for work on the site to finish. Brian readily agreed when Marjorie asked to leave early—to fetch her reinforcements, as it turned out—and in fact, he sent everyone else home a good twenty minutes before the usual time. Everyone, that is, except for John Ormerod. He and John had some extra work to see to, Brian had explained.

As arranged with Marjorie before she left the village, Christine hung around, out of sight of Brian and John, while the other workers set off for home. As soon as they disappeared round the bend of the road that led away from the village, Christine made off in the opposite direction, and worked her way round the bottom of the hill until she was just below the clump of bushes and the hiding-place. Marjorie, Graham and Peter had joined her there a few minutes later, and they had climbed the slope and positioned themselves ready for action.

It had already begun to grow dark, and Marjorie, acting as lookout, had to peer hard as she scanned the site for signs of movement. They had been waiting fifteen minutes or so when she suddenly hissed, "Here they are!" There was still enough light for Christine and the two boys to see two figures walking quickly across the village site. When they reached the centre, they paused and looked round, as if to check their position. Then Brian and John started towards the corner of the site near the hiding-place. Christine's heart turned over with trepidation.

"They've seen us! They know we're here!" she thought fearfully, but no, it was all right. Brian and John approached slowly, carefully surveying the ground in front of them. It was a tense moment. When the two of them came to a halt, they were only about ten metres from the hiding-place.

"It'll be here!" Christine heard Brian tell John in a loud whisper. "What luck!" he added, looking round. "It could have been anywhere, but it's on a part of the site we haven't excavated."

"I only hope you're right!" John muttered in reply. He seemed very tense and nervous, and kept surveying his surroundings as if to see that no one was watching.

"Little does he know!" Christine reflected.

Brian went over to him and gave him a push on the shoulder. "Come on, John! What are you waiting for? This is it!"

John managed to rouse himself, and Christine saw him give Brian a curt nod. The two of them began to dig, carefully turning back the earth with the spades they had brought with them. After turning a few clods of soil, they got down on their knees and began to work carefully with trowels. As they did so, Marjorie turned to her three companions and made the "get ready" signal. Christine tensed herself. Any moment now, she thought.

Just then, Christine heard John give a sharp cry. "Here! Brian! I've found it!" John had what looked to Christine like a small sack in his hands. He had just laid it carefully on the ground and with fingers trembling, began to open it, when Brian suddenly rushed forward and snatched it up.

"Now!" Marjorie hissed. "Come on—let's get 'em!" With Marjorie in the lead and Christine following behind, the Rawlings twins jumped up and hurtled towards John and Brian, who seemed transfixed with surprise for a moment. Before Brian knew what was happening, Peter Rawlings' had barged into him, knocking him flat on his back. The bag he had taken from John went flying, and Marjorie, seeing it, yelled to Christine,

"Grab it, Chris! Grab it!"

Christine responded at once, dodged round the spot where Brian and Peter were now locked in a vigorous struggle, and snatched up the bag. It was sticky in her hands and seemed to be made of very thick leather. As Christine clutched it close to her, to keep it safe, she felt something hard and round inside. Just then, Marjorie gave a loud shout.

"Oh, no you don't" she yelled. John was making for the spot where Christine stood when Marjorie flung herself at him and brought him crashing to the ground in a perfect rugby tackle. Christine gasped. Graham weighed in to help his sister, and before long John Ormerod was pinned down, utterly helpless. From what Christine could see of him, the expression on John's face was a mixture of amazement and fright.

Suddenly, there was a loud yell from nearby, and Christine

looked round to see, to her dismay, that Peter Rawlings was doubled up with pain on the ground. Brian was just scrambling to his feet. Brian must have been stronger than he looked, and had managed somehow to get a fist free and plant it in Peter's stomach. Peter's face was grey and he was groaning.

Brian, having freed himself, whirled round and shouted, "All right, you lot! Stop this! Christine, give that to me!" Christine felt a tight knot of fear inside. There, glinting out of the dark and pointing straight at her was the gun in Brian's hand.

"Give me that bag, Christine!" he repeated in a very menacing tone. "Come on now—move!"

Christine was trembling all over. She managed to stumble across to Brian and hand over the bag. She flinched back as he grabbed it from her and held it tight. There was a grim smile of satisfaction on his face.

"Now get back over there, with the others!" Brian ordered Christine. "And get those two on their feet," he went on, indicating John and Peter. "I want all of you where I can see you! You as well, John!"

John got slowly to his feet as Graham Rawlings went over to give Peter a hand. There was a look of stupefaction on his face.

"You had that gun on you all the time, Brian!" John gasped. "But why?" Brian gave a short laugh.

"You didn't really think I was going to share the treasure with you, did you John? If you did, then you're an even bigger fool than I thought!" Brian hugged the leather bag to him as he spoke. It must contain something very precious, Christine thought bleakly, thinking of the two ghost-children and their heartfelt pleadings.

"Don't look so amazed, John!" Brian sneered. "If you hadn't found the first box with half the rune message on it, you'd never have known a thing about the treasure, but I couldn't take the risk, you see, the risk that you'd find out those runes gave half of the instructions for where to find it."

"You wretch, you…" John had gone red in the face with fury and frustration. "I'll pay you back. You won't get away with this!"

She flinched back as he grabbed it from her and held it tight

Brian gave a cold smile. "Oh, yes I will!" he assured John. "But it was a close run thing, I'll admit that. I had to change my plans quickly after Christine here found the second box and you made your panic 'phone call in the middle of the night. I'd solved the rest of the rune message by that time, so I knew where the treasure was, and if you hadn't insisted on coming along to dig for the treasure tonight, I'd have done it by myself and been far away by this time!" Brian glowered, and waved the barrel of his gun so threateningly that Christine cowered back.

"Don't worry, my girl," Brian told her coolly. "I'm not in the business of shooting people unless I have to. But don't try any tricks! All I want is this." Once again, Brian hugged the leather bag. "It's mine and only mine. No one's going to cheat me of it now. I can live in luxury for the rest of my life."

"You'll live in prison for the rest of your life if you don't put that gun down—and quickly!"

The deep, commanding voice came out of the dark, making everyone jump, Brian King most of all. He went very pale, and turned just in time to see the tall burly policeman stride forward out of the shadows and grab his arm. The grip must have been very strong. Brian's face twisted up with pain, his hand opened and the policeman snatched up the gun.

There were three of them, three policemen who seemed to Christine to have materialised out of nowhere. She watched, open-mouthed as two of them pinned Brian's arms by his side. He tried to twist free, his face dark with fury, but they held him too tightly. The leather bag was on the ground nearby, and the first policeman picked it up and opened it.

It was quite dark by now, but as he drew the golden goblet out of the depths of the leather bag, the moonlight seemed to catch at it, and sparkle little glints of light off its surface. Everyone seemed to be mesmerised by the beautiful sight and for a good few seconds, no one moved or spoke.

At last, Christine gasped, "What is it? What is it?"

"The treasure of Our Lady of Easter, Chris!" It was Marjorie, her voice full of wonder. "That's what it is!" Marjorie came slowly forward and gazed at the goblet. Then, she grinned up at the policeman and Christine's eyes opened wider than ever when she suddenly flung her arms about him and kissed him.

"Well done, Constable!" Marjorie said in a mock pompous voice. "There could be promotion in this for you, you know!" Marjorie suddenly caught sight of Christine's astounded expression and laughed. "It's all right, Chris—I haven't gone off my rocker!" she said. "This is my other brother, Tom! I told you he'd be along later, didn't I!"

It was very cool and quiet inside the church. Christine and Marjorie paused as they entered, and savoured the calm, peaceful atmosphere before they began to walk towards the altar at the other end. Christine was carrying the two little boxes from the village site, and Marjorie, the splendid golden goblet. Now that it had been carefully cleaned, it shone and sparkled more brilliantly than ever.

When they had explained everything to the curator at the Lady of Easter Museum, he had agreed that the treasures should not be put on display there. Their rightful place was in the church. Still, Christine could not help thinking that, for all their beauty and great value, these objects had caused a great deal of trouble and distress. Because of them, Brian King was now serving a prison sentence for theft and threats with an offensive weapon. John Ormerod, being only sixteen, had got off with a very severe reprimand. Even so, everyone in Eyemouth knew what he had done, and he could not escape the shame and embarrassment of it. Christine felt Marjorie give her a nudge.

"Go on, Chris!" she said quietly. "You're the one to do it!"

Marjorie was holding out the goblet and Christine took it. She stepped forward and placed the treasures on the altar.

As she did so, Christine half expected to feel or hear something which would tell her that the two ghost-children were around. Then, she realised. The task which those two tiny children had begun over a thousand years ago was now complete. Eostre had her treasures once more. The ghost-children would never been seen again.

Corfu Conspiracy

by JACKIE KEMP

Melanie could hardly believe that just five days ago she had been drooping moodily around, convalescing from a bad bout of glandular fever. She had missed her school sports day and the class outing and felt left out of everything.

Then came the evening everything had changed. Melanie had been watching television when she heard her parents in the dining-room. She caught the end of her father's sentence.

"... to Corfu this time ... for about eighteen days."

Lucky Dad, so he was off on business again. Melanie knew that his work as a food research chemist meant going all over the world. A Greek island, though. Then came his next words.

"It's a shame Melanie isn't well enough, she could have come with me." Not well enough! Melanie was off the settee, through the door and in the dining-room in five seconds flat.

Her pleading led to a visit to her doctor, who Melanie felt like hugging when he said that the dry heat would be good for her. Mum was to follow them in five or six days, since her job as a school secretary meant that she had to wait for the end of term.

So here she sat, waiting for take-off to Corfu. The Captain spoke, they had flight clearance. Melanie was much too excited to be nervous, the engines roared, one minute they were taxiing down the runway, then there was a bump and they were up!

They were circling over Corfu

It seemed that she barely had time to eat her meal when they were circling over Corfu. A green, brown and white drop set amidst a sparkling turquoise and blue sea.

As they stepped from the plane the heat hit them. Melanie was glad to get through customs and out into the sunshine. Dad's hired car was waiting and they were soon off. The winding road they took led them past long beaches, hotels, tumble-down cottages, and many tavernas with tables outside. They were going to be staying at a taverna, and when they arrived they were greeted by Elena, a smiling Greek woman.

The meal that first evening was one that Melanie would always remember. They sat outside the taverna at a table covered by a snowy-white tablecloth. Above them, ripening grapes hung from a wooden trellis, forming a fragrant canopy.

The food tasted out of this world. Melanie had kebabs, spicy meat balls, chips cooked to perfection in olive oil and a deliciously dressed Greek salad. She was in bed by ten o'clock and slept more soundly than she had done for weeks. She awoke to a cloudless blue sky and an invitation for an early morning swim from her father.

He stayed around the taverna that first day, but that evening he told her that he would have to work the next day. Melanie did not mind, she was quite happy being just thirty metres from the beach and those warm crystal-clear waters.

For the next few days Melanie swam and sunbathed quite happily while her father went off working. He rarely spoke about his job since it tended to be very technical, yet one evening a few days later he said,

"I've been doing some soil tests up in the hills in an old olive grove. It's a funny thing you know, the grove is owned by an old lady and her olives are the best on the island. I'm trying to find out why. She's a true Greek widow, dressed all in black. She thinks my tests are a bit of a joke, but she's got two grandsons who don't think I'm at all amusing. They follow me everywhere and hide when I turn round. Anyway I should be finished up there tomorrow, then I can take some time off."

The next day was very hot, not a breath of air stirred the olive trees on the hills behind the taverna. Melanie left the beach early, for once it was too hot for her. She had a lazy nap, then showered, changed and went down to the front of the taverna to wait for her father. By half past eight it was getting dark and he still had not returned. She found Elena.

"I'm a bit worried about my father," she said. Elena replied with her habitual shrug of the shoulders.

"Maybe he stay late" she said busily preparing the evening meals. Melanie felt guilty bothering her and went back to her table. By ten o'clock she had eaten a lonely meal and was quite concerned about him, so she went in search of Elena again. This time she agreed to telephone the hospital. Picking up the telephone she jiggled the receiver rest up and down frowning.

"'s not working again." Then she saw Melanie's face and smiled. "I send Andreas, he be back very soon. You see."

As the waiter took off on his scooter, Melanie was more concerned that he would get there and back in one piece, he zoomed off so fast, but he was back within an hour. No there had been "No Eengleeshman" taken to the hospital today.

"There you see ... no need for worry. He not have accident, he stay at his work for the night," smiled Elena.

"But I'm sure he would have telephoned," said Melanie.

"No. Telephone not work," replied Elena, sounding final. She did have a point, but still it was not like her dad. It was a worried Melanie who went to bed and eventually fell into a restless sleep.

She awoke the next morning with a funny feeling in the pit of her stomach, and for a moment could not think why. Then she remembered! She dressed quickly and hurried to his room. His bed had obviously not been slept in, and Elena confirmed that he had not come back during the night. Elena still was not worried and insisted that he had probably stayed at work. Melanie ate her breakfast mechanically, her mind busy working. She knew the name of the village where her father had been working and she had a description of the old lady. She decided to brave the Greek bus service and go to the village.

"Excuse me," she said. "My father, Mr Campbell, is he here?"

The bus to Corfu town was only a little late and when she got to the bus station a scene of total chaos met her. Buses parking, reversing and leaving, horns blaring, people everywhere, shouting, running, laughing and above it all a wailing voice. Melanie strained her ears to hear. It sounded for all the world like "Doughnuts", and so it was! A stooping old man was selling large ring-shaped doughnuts from a wooden tray. She could not resist them and bought two. As she stood biting into the warm, deliciously sugary doughnut, studying the bus timetable on a board, she almost forgot her worries. However, if the times were right the bus she wanted was leaving any minute. She ran along the line of buses searching for the right one. There! It looked very full, but the doors were still open, and as she hesitated on the platform, a large man behind her gave her an impatient shove into the bus and clambered on after her.

There could not possibly be room, but Melanie had reckoned without the Greek conductor's apparent lack of concern for the comfort of his passengers. He shoved the rest of the standing passengers further down the bus, yelling and waving his arms rudely. Good grief! There were at least twenty-five people standing. No one seemed to care though, so she grabbed the nearest seat-back and prepared for a long uncomfortable ride.

When she eventually reached the tiny village, the owner of a taverna gave her directions to the old lady's vineyard and after a short walk she found the house.

Melanie was so busy looking at the pretty white-washed house, that for a minute she did not notice the old lady herself sitting on the verandah. She fitted Dad's description exactly, and was watching Melanie closely. Melanie coughed.

"Excuse me," she said. "My father, Mr Campbell, is he here?" Melanie held her breath waiting for the answer.

"Your father?" The old lady spoke good English, "Mr Campbell?" She raised her eyebrows. "No, he went early yesterday."

"You're quite sure?" asked Melanie. "It's just that he did not come back to the taverna last night, and I'm very worried."

"One moment, my child," and the old woman stood up and

called, "Nikos, Spiro." Melanie guessed that these were her grandsons. A few minutes later a surly-looking Greek appeared.

"Ah Spiro, this young lady she look for her father, the scientist man Campbell. Has he been here today?"

The young man flicked his dark eyes at Melanie, she could see surprise and something else in them, quite what she could not say. She shivered.

"No, grandmother. He finished work yesterday," and after another look in Melanie's direction, he turned and left.

"You see my child. He is not here. I am so sorry."

Melanie did not wait. She thanked the old lady and turned away. She planned to follow Spiro, knowing what Dad had said about the man's strange behaviour. She had watched him leave and once out of sight of the old lady, she turned and hurried after him. The trees hid her and after a few hundred metres she heard voices and crept towards the sounds. Luck was with her: there were Spiro and another Greek talking. Spiro was clearly telling his brother about her, but he did not seem to think it was worth worrying. He just shrugged his shoulders.

They turned and moved off through the trees and Melanie followed at a safe distance. After some minutes they stopped by an old, gnarled olive tree. She ducked down behind a bush of fragrant wild rosemary, then shifted to get comfortable. When she looked again they had disappeared. Where on earth were they? She waited. Then, just as she was about to move nearer to the tree, Nikos' head appeared, as if by magic, beside the tree.

"What on earth?" thought Melanie. The rest of Nikos came into view, as he clambered up from somewhere underground. He paused and spoke to someone down below. Then he moved something heavy on the ground and strode off.

She waited for about ten minutes but nothing happened, so she crept towards the old tree. She could see nothing, so she bent down to look more carefully. Still nothing, but there must be, she thought. Then she noticed a slab of stone right by the tree trunk, partly hidden by the long grass. So this was what Nikos was moving! There was a heavy ring embedded in the stone. Melanie did not dare try to move it knowing that Spiro was underneath so she crept back to her hiding-place to wait.

Her brain was pounding. She closed her eyes to think. The sun was making speckled patterns on her eyelids where it filtered through the trees. It was so warm. The next thing she knew was the sound of voices. Glancing at her watch she could hardly believe she had slept for an hour. She peeked out, Spiro was waiting by the tree and Nikos was walking back with a tall, worried-looking stranger. Melanie could hear him speaking. He was an American.

"Yeah you're right, Nikos, we'll have to keep the guy here till we get it out of Greece. Real bad luck him finding the grotto like that. Coupla days later and we'd have got it away and no one any the wiser. You're sure his car's hidden good?" The Greeks nodded and after shaking hands the American added, "Okay, Nikos, get it to that cove by dawn. I'll have the money."

As the three men walked away Melanie's brain was in turmoil. The "he" must be her father! It had to be. She waited until they were well away then ran to the tree. She grasped the ring in the stone and pulled. She could not move it. She pulled again, but still it did not budge.

She sat with her back against the tree trunk. What should she do next? What was hidden underground? As she moved her head a little, a feathery grass touched her nose and she sneezed. In the following stillness she distinctly heard a faint voice from behind her. It seemed to be coming from the tree.

"Hello," she said, feeling rather foolish to be talking to a tree. This time the voice was louder, puzzled and familiar!

"Melanie?"

"Yes it's me, Dad. Where on earth are you?"

"Never mind that. Can you move the slab?"

"No, I've tried can't budge it."

"Okay, good girl. Now listen." Then as quickly as he could he told Melanie what had happened.

While he was taking samples from this very tree he had discovered the slab. The two brothers seemed nowhere around, although he was mistaken as he later found out. He had moved the slab and discovered steps leading down to a grotto. The sides of the steps went right by the tree roots, which was how they could talk. In the grotto he had found a beautiful statue of Saint Spiridon, the patron saint of Corfu. He had just discovered that the statue was probably gold, when everything had gone black! When he came to, he was tied hand and foot.

"I don't know what they're up to, or how long they planned to keep me here." Melanie told her father what she had overheard.

"Ah, so that's it. The American's buying it. I don't suppose the Greek government would pay them enough. It's up to us then. This statue belongs in Greece, not abroad. Now listen. Go back to the taverna, get Elena and tell the police. You'd better bang on the trunk of the tree when you get back, then if I don't call out, you'll know they're down here."

After a quick goodbye Melanie sped off. She took a backward look, yes, she could find the tree again. Luckily the bus to Corfu town was late, and although it was as chaotic as ever, she reached the taverna safely.

Elena listened wide-eyed to Melanie's story and for once she did not shrug her shoulders, but sent Andreas for the police. When they arrived Elena spoke rapidly to them.

"You show us the place." It was an order. Melanie got into the car with the four burly Greek policemen, and they were off.

That drive along those winding Greek roads was one that Melanie would never forget, no matter how hard she tried! Horn blaring, one minute leaping forward, the next braking violently to avoid an oncoming car or bus. As they approached the village they slowed to a saner speed, and she directed them to the vineyard. Then all but the driver got out, and he drove quietly off, Melanie assumed to hide the car somewhere. She led them through the trees and as they approached the old tree she noticed all three policemen had drawn their guns. She shivered. When she banged on the tree her father gave the all clear.

The policemen moved the stone as if it were cardboard. They went rapidly down the steps, waving at Melanie to stay where

She brushed the tears of relief from her cheeks and smiled

she was. She did so, shivering. Then her father called her,

"Come on, Melanie." A torch lit the steps and the next moment she was in her father's arms.

"Hey, steady on, Melanie. Mind my poor head!" She brushed the tears of relief from her cheeks and smiled. The biggest of the policemen stopped any further conversation.

"We trap these men. We wait down here for them with Mr Campbell. Miss, you have to wait here too. Be very quiet." So she was to see the capture! They hid Melanie behind a rock and then they all settled down to wait. Once the slab was back in place it was pitch black. They waited, and waited, until quite suddenly moonlight shone into the grotto and Melanie saw two figures silhouetted against the bright night sky: Nikos and Spiro, it had to be. They came right down the steps and straight into the arms of the policemen. There was hardly a struggle.

Melanie had a minute or two to admire the beautiful statue, then the brothers were led away, the grotto was sealed and guarded and she and her father were taken back to the taverna.

The next day the police called to bring back Melanie's father's car. It had been as they had thought. Spiros had found the statue some weeks earlier and he and Nikos planned to sell it to the American for much more money than their own government would pay them. The old lady had known nothing and was apparently very upset about her grandsons' unpatriotic behaviour. The brothers were being "dealt with". Melanie did not ask how. The American had disappeared and Mel was to receive a reward from the Greek government: free holidays in Greece whenever they wanted. It was all too good to be true.

"That'll be something to tell Mum," said her father. Heavens, Mum! Melanie had almost forgotten with all the excitement, that she was due in that afternoon. They met her at the airport. After she had hugged Melanie, she said,

"You do look well. I can see your Dad's really been looking after you." At that, Melanie opened her mouth to protest, then caught her father's eye. At which point they both burst out laughing. What a lot they had to tell her!

Jump for Joy

by GEOFFREY MORGAN

"Good heavens!" exclaimed Sally Lawton, indignantly. "You're not going to back out now, are you?"

Joy Marlowe looked up and gave her friend a sickly imitation of a smile.

"Of course I'm not—if I can help it," she added, defensively. "The trouble is I don't think Sambo's in a jumping mood today." She looked at the shapely figure of her pony with an admiring and affectionate eye; but Sambo ignored the remarks and the look, and went on cropping the grass in the shadow of the horsebox from which Joy had just unloaded him.

"You mean you're not in a jumping mood," retorted Sally without sympathy. She cast an appraising glance at the pony. "He's never looked so fit, and provided you don't let him swallow the whole meadow he should carry you to victory."

The truth was, of course, as Sally well knew, this was the first agricultural show and gymkhana in which Joy was taking an active part, and she was a little scared of making a fool of herself before a critical audience over the jumps in the grand ring.

"Snap out of it, Joy." Sally tried to look confident. "I know how you feel. I felt the same way before my first performance with the dramatic club—first night nerves. Once you're in the ring, those jumps will just melt before your eyes."

"If anything's going to melt before four o'clock this afternoon it'll be me," Joy murmured, dabbing the back of her neck.

"Better keep in the shade then," advised Sally gently, squinting up at the bright morning sun through a leafy pattern of elm branches. "We don't want you to get sunstroke."

Before Joy could voice a suitable reply to her friend's unselfish remark, a strong boyish voice bade them good morning. They spun round to find a smart youngster with a conceited grin on his face, sitting astride a handsome chestnut pony. He looked loftily down on them, but in spite of that Sally returned his greeting. The boy glanced from Sally to the grazing pony.

"Are you in the jumps this afternoon?" he asked.

"No," she indicated Joy, "but my friend is." He looked at Joy. Although he was younger than the two girls he was obviously pretending that he was their senior and the more experienced.

"Have you had a look at the jumps?" he inquired of Joy.

"No," returned Joy curtly. "Why?"

"I thought they looked pretty stiff."

"Did you?" she queried, and wondered why she felt so hot when she was standing in the shade.

"I thought so," said boy loftily, "but then I think you always do till you actually take them, don't you?"

Joy suddenly found she was having difficulty in swallowing and while she was trying to overcome this, Sally replied,

"Well, it really depends on one's experience," she answered brightly. "After a spot of rough riding you take little things like that in your stride." The boy's eyebrows arched slightly.

"Are you a rough rider?" he asked stiffly.

"Well, no, I'm not. Not really. But my friend here has ridden in practically every position."

He smiled. "I hope she manages to retain a dignified position this afternoon," he said. "Good luck, anyway." He rode off smartly, the competition number strapped to the back of his riding jacket waving a mock farewell.

"He's a little swank!" muttered Joy. "Who is he, anyway? His face looks familiar. I'm sure I know him."

"Have you had a look at the jumps?" he inquired of Joy

"I've seen him somewhere," mused Sally, "but I don't know his name."

"Well, what are we waiting for?" Joy suddenly exclaimed. "His number's thirty-six. He must be in the programme." She took the crumpled leaflet from her pocket and turned the pages.

"Is he in the jumping event?" demanded Sally.

"He's in nearly every event," Joy muttered, her eyes running down the entry list. "He must be a real little expert. Number thirty-six," she read aloud. "Jerry Hutton on Saywen." She gazed dismally across the park in the direction Master Hutton had gone, and Sally snatched the programme and began to read the list of entries for the jumping competition.

"I've got it, Sally," Joy exclaimed. "I know where I've seen him. His photo was in the *Mercury* two weeks ago—after the Belmont Show. Don't you remember, he won most of the prizes and made the other competitors look silly? The paper called him Jumping Jerry!" Sally looked as perturbed as her friend.

"That's right. I remember now," she frowned. "But don't worry, Joy, the paper's bound to exaggerate. He can't be all that good or he wouldn't have thought our jumps were stiff. Cheer up and come and drink an ice-cream soda."

"I'm not going to the refreshment tents, I don't feel sociable," Joy returned moodily. "Let's go over to Daddy's stand and have a drink in the caravan." She asked the horsebox driver to keep an eye on Sambo, and they moved off.

"Well, there is one consolation, anyway," observed Sally, brightly. "If Jumping Jerry gets through all the events he's down for he'll be exhausted by the time he comes to the jumps!"

"You can tell that to the *Mercury*," Joy retorted without much enthusiasm as they headed towards the machinery stands.

Runsdale Agricultural Show was held annually in a pleasant stretch of Hampshire parkland which formed part of Lord Alton's estate. He was president of the Runsdale Agricultural Club and loaned the best part of his delightful grounds free for the important occasion, and so about the middle of June each year his lush meadows became the setting for throngs of gaily dressed people who wandered along the avenues of exhibitors' stands and displays and clustered around the refreshment marquees.

Joy's father had had an implement stand on the showground each year since the foundation of the club, and Joy had attended the annual event from the time she had learned to walk; but she had never been a competitor in the show ring. This year, encouraged by her father, and Sally's enthusiasm for her riding ability, she had impulsively added her name to the list of entries; but now that the time had come to display her horsemanship she was about as keen to enter the ring as a cat is to enter water.

It was not many months ago that she had completed her first riding lessons and but six weeks since her father had presented her with Sambo, and frankly, the few jumps they had been over together were small compared with the number they had negotiated separately, though Joy had not intended it that way. Now, to cap all her fears, she found she was competing against a boy who was so good that the press called him Jumping Jerry!

The ice-cream soda in the quiet comfort of the caravan tucked away behind the marquee on Mr Marlowe's machinery stand did nothing to dispel the mounting gloom that enveloped her. The murmur of the crowds, the crackling voice from the public address speakers, and the rumble of farm machinery that were working exhibits, penetrated the oppressive silence of the mobile lounge like the distant roll of thunder.

"Wish it would rain," Joy said, with sudden fervour. "What wouldn't I give to see a solid downpour for the rest of the day!"

"Wouldn't make a scrap of difference to the events in the ring," replied Sally, knowingly. "The show would go on."

"I know, but the ring would be in an awful mess, and Sambo won't jump at all on soft ground."

Sally shook her head sympathetically. "No use wishing, Joy. It won't rain today."

Joy was still wishing, however, as the hands of the clock in the wooden tower near the ring crept towards three-thirty. She had to admit Sally was right, though, it would not rain. The sky

"Wish it would rain," Joy said, with sudden fervour

was the same azure blue and the sun beat down unmercifully as she reined in Sambo in the shade of a tree.

For the past half an hour she had been giving her pony some gentle exercise in the more isolated stretches of the park, and now as she sat in the saddle, dabbing her moist forehead, she suddenly realised she was looking over a low boundary hedge into the private gardens of Runsdale Manor. Beyond the hedge a smooth lawn lay between her and the rather gaunt 17th-century house. Thick shrubs lined the path which led up to a shallow terrace from a wicket gate in the hedge just to her left.

While she gazed absently at the material evidence of Lord Alton's wealth, her mind was obsessed with an imaginative picture which featured herself and Sambo limping round the ring knocking down each jump in turn. She could hear the loud-speakers telling the crowd that number thirty-seven had gained every fault in the book! She had just reached the stage where she was running Sambo out of the ring to the accompaniment of derisive clapping and laughter, when a movement behind one of the first floor windows of the house suddenly demanded her concentrated attention.

From the leafy screen of the tree she had a clear view while remaining hidden herself, and she guessed the windows she was now watching were those of the main bedrooms. They were tall casement windows overlooking a flat roof which extended over a large room below, which jutted out on to the terrace in the form of a loggia.

Joy waited. The show and the ring and the distant noise of people and machinery were forgotten.

Presently, the curtain was drawn aside and one of the windows slowly opened. A man's head appeared, moving cautiously from side to side, the eyes obviously searching the gardens. The next moment the window was opened wide and the figure swung himself over the sill and dropped lightly to the flat roof. He turned and closed the window behind him. He was quaintly dressed in a cloth cap, riding jacket and breeches and a pair of light rubber-soled shoes. From where Joy was they looked like running shoes. It was obvious from the man's appearance and furtive actions that he had no right to be in Runsdale Manor.

Joy silently dismounted, tethered Sambo to a low branch of the tree and crept to the hedge for a closer view. She watched while the man dropped from the loggia roof to the ground and hurried along the path, keeping close to the shrubs. He opened the wicket gate and ran off to the left slap into a cluster of rhododendron bushes. He disappeared from view. Joy waited but there was no sign of her quarry appearing from the further side of the bush, so she moved forward to investigate.

She edged herself cautiously into the bushes and then stood still, hardly daring to breathe, for there in a gap in the centre of the shrub, was the man struggling into a pair of riding boots!

He had thrown off his cloth cap and now that Joy could see him at close quarters she realised he was no more than three or four years older than herself. It was obvious that the stranger, disguised to look as though he was taking part in the show, was nothing more than a common thief using the show as a cover.

Joy considered the situation urgently. The ring, the crowds and the police were not far away. She heard the loudspeakers blaring and guessed the annoucer was calling up the competitors for the jumping events. Could she get to one of the policemen before the young man had a chance of getting out of the park? She was not given time to make up her mind, for the next moment the fellow had pulled on his boots, kicked his running shoes under the foliage and was pushing his way out.

There was only one thing to do to stop him—and Joy did it. As the stranger emerged, she crept from her hiding-place, stepped up behind him and brought the hard end of her riding-crop down on his head. There was a faint groan and he reeled back against the bush, collapsing silently among the flowers.

As Joy tried to tug him out on to the turf her hand felt a hard package in the inside pocket of his riding jacket. The young man began to moan and his eyelids flickered; but Joy did not ask any questions. She thrust her hand into his pocket and drew out a soft leather bag. From inside she pulled out a neck-

Her victim struggled dazedly to a sitting position

lace of stones that flashed sparkles of fire in the sunlight. There were several other necklaces, as well as rings and bracelets.

Joy did not know much about jewellery, but she did know enough to recognise expensive diamonds when she saw them, and knowing where the youth had been she had no doubts as to how valuable they were. She stuffed the bag into her pocket and raced across to Sambo while her victim struggled dazedly to a sitting position. Throwing herself into the saddle she coaxed Sambo across the springy turf like the wind.

As she approached the ring she heard the announcer's voice, "Number Thirty-six, Jerry Hutton on Saywen. Two faults."

Joy dimly recollected that she was next on the entry list, then promptly dismissed the fact in her urgency to find a policeman. She urged Sambo towards the competitors' enclosure which adjoined the ring. There was usually a policeman at the gate, but not this time. Sally was there, however, looking around her in desperation. As soon as she saw Joy she ran to meet her.

"Where's your number?" she demanded. "You're in next. Jumpy Jerry didn't get a clear round." Joy's number card was sticking out of her pocket. Sally snatched it, tying it around her friend's waist. "You've got a good chance," she cried. "Jerry's knocked some bricks off the wall, and no one's gone clear—"

"Stop nagging," cut in Joy, "and find a policeman. I've just caught a crook leaving the manor with a diamond necklace and a bag of jewellery."

"This is no time to be funny," retorted Sally fiercely. "You've got to go through with it now. They're calling your number."

"But it's the truth, I tell you!" cried Joy, desperately. "I've got the diamonds in my pocket. Look!" She suddenly pointed across the park. "There's a bobby, and see, beyond him—the man near the hedge—that's the thief who stole the diamonds...."

"All right, all right," interrupted Sally gently, grabbing the reins and trying to humour her. "Give me the diamonds, Joy. I'll take them to the police officer. I'll do anything," she went on soothingly, "if you'll only get into the ring!"

"Tell him where they came from and get him to arrest that

young man in riding kit before he gets away." Joy dropped the leather bag into Sally's hands and rode into the enclosure.

Sally opened the bag in a daze—and then nearly fainted.

"Gosh!" she gasped aloud though no one was in earshot. "They are diamonds!" She turned abruptly and began running towards the policeman.

Joy swept into the ring and started her run almost before she was given the starting signal. She did not know how she managed to clear the first three obstacles—a brush fence, a gate and a stile—but the short bursts of applause told her she must have done so.

As she turned to be begin her run before the next three jumps, she was just able to see Sally walking quickly away with the police officer, obviously going in the direction the young crook had taken. With her mind ranging out ahead of her it was not surprising that Sambo knocked a great chunk out of the dummy wall, hit the gate for six and dropped the top two crossbars of the wooden fence! The crowd roared with laughter.

Joy clenched her teeth and turned Sambo to take the last two jumps in the centre of the ring. Somehow they both managed to scrape over these together without knocking them down, and then they were galloping out of the ring. As they reached the enclosure the announcer's voice boomed out, "Number Thirty-seven, Joy Marlowe on Sambo. Twelve faults."

At any other time Joy's face would have turned a carnation red at this blatant announcement; but she was not concerned with the competition now. She was looking across the parkland for Sally and the constable. It was not until she and Sambo were out of the enclosure that she saw them—and she was very puzzled. They were moving away towards the boundary of the park. Beyond the shallow hedge they were approaching, a broad meadow inclined upwards to end in a tall bush fence behind which Joy glimpsed the shiny roof of a car. She decided it must be waiting in the narrow lane which led on to the main road a couple of kilometres away. Forcing his way through the hedge towards the car was the thief in the riding outfit.

The next moment the whole sequence of events formed a clear picture in Joy's mind, for there was wild shriek from Sally, a brief struggle between her and the constable, and then the latter was racing off across the meadow, his helmet rolling on the ground as he ran.

"Stop, thief! Stop, thief!" Joy's voice shrilled out lustily. Pointing her riding crop at the running figure of the police officer, she spurred Sambo forward. Her warning cries had not been in vain. A couple of men on horses swung round and began to follow her. A police motor-cyclist was threading his way out of the crowd. Relieved she was getting help at last, Joy urged Sambo on. They went over the shallow hedge in fine style and found Sally scrambling to her feet on the other side.

"He's a fake!" cried Sally, breathlessly, pointing an accusing finger after the man in uniform. "And he's taken the diamonds!"

Joy nodded and, pressing her knees into Sambo's flanks, they galloped on. The man in the uniform of the law was forcing his way through the bush fence now and Joy knew that if she was going to prevent the thieves' escape she and Sambo had got to jump the high sprawling hedge together. This was the supreme test of her riding skill. She crouched low over the pony's neck and then momentarily closed her eyes.

She could not be quite certain what happened in the next few whirling seconds. She was vaguely aware of the youth bent over the steering wheel of the car, of the sound of a motor-cycle in the lane, of the man she had chased slowly rising from his knees after crawling out of the hedge. Then she was conscious of a violent shaking as Sambo stumbled on landing. She suddenly became airborne—and then thudded down on to the back of the escaping crook. The impact sent the man down with Joy on top, the girl receiving a crack on the chin from her quarry's head as they sprawled across the ground.

In an unpleasant daze Joy was helped to her feet. The confusing scene with police, crooks and spectators was spinning giddily before her. She was dimly aware of Sally supporting her, and cheerfully murmuring in her ear, "No one's seen a jump

Sally stared at her. "You mean it was an accident?"

like that before, Joy. You were marvellous!" And on that proud note the scene, so far as Joy was concerned, faded altogether.

Sally was not alone in her praise. The *Mercury* joined in with banner headlines the next day. The editor had devoted half of his front page to Joy's gallant display of horsemanship in which she had brought about the capture of the jewel thieves. There were photographs of Sambo and Joy, and Joy and Sally, but none of Jumping Jerry.

Joy was standing by the window in her father's study searching the paper in vain for a reference to her shameful display in the ring when Sally entered, brandishing another copy of the paper in her waving hands.

"You know you're front page news this morning, Joy," she said with a hint of envy. "The ring displays were chicken-feed compared with your leap from the saddle on to the back of this crook, Hardwick. It says as much here." She tapped the paper.

"I didn't intend to do it, you know," admitted Joy, candidly.

Sally stared at her. "You mean, it was an accident?"

Joy nodded. "It was. Sambo stumbled. I went over his head. It was just pure luck I happened to land on Hardwick."

"Well, accident or not, you were responsible for retrieving Lady Alton's diamonds," Sally replied stoutly. "There are rumours that Lord Alton is going to offer you a reward."

Joy folded the newspaper. "If he does, I won't accept it."

"What?" gasped Sally, incredulously.

"I've got a better plan." Joy spoke quietly but there was a twinkle in her eyes. "I shall ask him for a silver cup to become known as the Marlowe Cup which I can present each year to the winner of the jumping competition."

Sally scratched the tip of her nose. "I see," she murmured, her eyes narrowing. "You couldn't possibly compete for your own cup so there'd be no chance of spoiling the build-up the paper's given you today."

"That's partly the idea," Joy agreed, smiling. The other part is that it's more comfortable presenting a cup than jumping for it!" and she sat down very gingerly in a well-cushioned chair.

Another World Away

by BRENDA RALPH LEWIS

Any moment now, the guardian robots would be coming for her. Miranda had been in the judgement cell for long enough to recognise the warning signs. First, the steady hum of the mind-searcher stopped. A second or two later, the beams which stretched across the entrance to the judgement room like invisible bars, would be switched off, and the corridor outside would no longer appear to be flickering and waving in the heat they emanated. Next would come the metallic tramp of the robots' feet, taking her... Where? Miranda wondered. Where would the robots take her this time? To the Young Judge, the one with the cold eyes and the bullying manner? Or to the Old Judge, who spoke more softly and gave Miranda the strange impression that he was trying to help her explain why she had committed the crime of disobedience?

Whichever one it was, Miranda trusted neither of them. Both Judges were in the business of ensuring that Pax City remained peaceful and orderly beneath its huge artificially-ventilated dome. It had always been so, ever since the great System Analyst Kremlin and his computer team created it, a century ago, in the year 2110. To ensure it remained that way, and that the absolute obedience to authority which made it possible was maintained, Miranda knew that both Judges would be willing to execute her or have her exiled to the prison planet far out in deep space. In fact, it was well known that most culprits who appeared before the Old Judge for crimes of disobedience were never seen again, and no one knew what happened to them.

The trouble was, though, that Miranda could not explain why she had disobeyed the Work Officer, or why she had protested so strongly when he punished Dierdre for doing bad work in the factory. It was not as if Miranda liked Dierdre all that much.

Perhaps it had been the sight of Dierdre cringing and crying as the Work Officer pointed the pain wand at her that had made Miranda act as she did. All she remembered was hearing the drone of the level one beam as it leapt out of the wand and struck Dierdre with all-over prickling like a million hot, stabbing needles. Dierdre fell to the floor, whimpering, and either could not or would not get to her feet when the Work Officer told her to do so. The Work Officer was just tuning the pain wand to the infinitely more agonising level two when Miranda suddenly found herself leaping at him. Spreading her hand out, she planted it in his face. The officer staggered, but Miranda, pushing with a strength she did not know she possessed, off-balanced him and sent him crashing to the floor.

"You bully, you rotten bully!" Miranda yelled, not caring that her furious words could be heard right across the factory floor. "If you showed Dierdre how to operate that machine, she might learn how to do it properly! The pain wand won't make her work better. You're as bad as the robots! They can't think or feel and neither can you!"

Miranda was so completely gripped by her anger that she even made a dive for the pain wand, which had fallen to the floor in the struggle, intending to give the Work Officer a taste of it, but he had been too quick for her, and scrambled up just in time to snatch it from her grasp and press the signal button on his uniform that summoned the guardian robots. They had arrived immediately, their square, blank faces flickering the three red warning lights that denoted they were hurrying to an emergency. It had all been over quickly after that. The robots' metal fingers gripped Miranda's arms and held her helpless.

"To the judgement room!" snapped the Work Officer, realising that only the Judges could handle an offence as serious as the one Miranda had committed. The robots transported Miranda to the judgement room immediately, and Dierdre with her. Miranda could hear Dierdre now, as she huddled in the opposite corner of the room crying and snivelling in her usual fashion. Miranda glanced at her, and felt a moment of dislike. There was nothing to commend Dierdre to anyone: she was untidy, surly, always complaining. Why, why had Miranda risked her very existence for the sake of this unattractive little girl?

Miranda tussled with the problem for hours on end. Over and over again, she relived in her mind the events of that fateful afternoon in the factory, but all she remembered was an overwhelming feeling of injustice, and the certainty that the Work Officer had been wrong and cruel to treat Dierdre as he did.

"But surely, I was wrong?" Miranda murmured to herself. "Surely Dierdre deserved the punishment?" At least this sort of thinking was acceptable to the mindsearcher which, as Miranda well knew, was reading and recording her thoughts on the judgement computer.

Miranda was abruptly roused from her thoughts by the sound of metallic clanking. The guardian robots had arrived. In a moment, they appeared, with alternate red and green lights flashing on their face-dials, indicating a command to Miranda and Dierdre to follow them. To Miranda's dismay, the mere sight of the robots set Dierdre screaming with fright.

"No, no! Go away! I won't come with you! Go away!" Dierdre was curling herself up in the corner as if attempting to melt through the walls in order to elude the robots. Immediately, a jagged red line began to flicker across the robots' face-dials. Miranda knew that signal—it was the signal for anger—and robots programmed to become angry as these guardians were could be very formidable opponents. Dierdre had only made things worse by her outburst. The two robots began tramping towards her. Dierdre turned terribly white.

"After all, they're only heaps of metal and wire!"

"She's only a kid, a poor frightened kid!" Miranda thought.

Suddenly, she was striding across the room just in time to place herself between the cringing Dierdre and the advancing robots. They lumbered a couple of paces more, then stopped, sensing the obstruction. Their face-dials went blank for a second or two. Then, a circle of lights began revolving. That meant comprehension signals were speeding along their integrated circuits, seeking instructions from the judgement computer as to what they should do next. The computer would answer in moments, Miranda knew.

"Stop this, do you hear?" she told Dierdre in an urgent voice. "It's no good defying the robots. You should know that!"

"I don't want to come. Tell them to go away, please, Miranda, please!" Dierdre was sobbing with fear now.

"I can't, I can't!" Miranda was feeling desperate now. "Look, Dierdre, we must behave with…" Miranda searched for the right word, "with dignity," she said. "Show them we're not afraid of them. After all," Miranda went on, glaring the robots in the face-dials. "They're only heaps of metal and wire! Come on, Dierdre!" she added kindly.

"Well, if you'll hold my hand, I might feel better!" Dierdre told her in a whisper, holding out a small, grimy hand. Miranda took it. It was ice cold. She helped Dierdre to her feet, though the poor child was still so frightened that she could hardly stand. Miranda put one arm around her to support her, and she felt Dierdre clinging to her as if she was her last hope.

"All right," Miranda told the robots. "We're ready now!"

As Miranda, still with her arm around Dierdre, entered the judgement hall in the wake of the robots, she realised that this was the occasion she had been dreading all along. Both the Young Judge and the Old Judge were seated at the table. That could mean only one thing—they were going to pronounce sentence. In a few moments, Miranda and Dierdre would know what their punishment was to be. Miranda swallowed hard, trying to contain her own fear. For Dierdre's sake, she felt she must do her best to put a brave face on things.

As soon as the Young Judge saw the two girls he turned to the robots with a short, sharp command.

"Make them stand apart!" he snapped, his eyes cold as they always were. The robots, obedient, moved towards Miranda and Dierdre, their metal arms spread out to pull the two of them away from each other.

"No, leave them as they are!" It was the Old Judge. His younger companion looked at him in surprise. "It will not make any difference to their punishment," the Old Judge explained. "Justice in Pax City is quite hard enough. We do not have to be cruel as well!"

The Young Judge frowned and clicked his teeth with annoyance, but out of respect for his older colleague, Miranda imagined, he said nothing.

The two Judges had drawn lots before Miranda and Dierdre arrived, and it was the Young Judge's turn to speak his decision first.

"We have considered the matter very carefully," he told the two girls. "There is no doubt that both of you are guilty of disobedience and rebellion. It would seem," the Young Judge went on, looking lofty and pompous, "that you have forgotten why we live as we do in Pax City. I will tell you!"

Out of the corner of her eye, Miranda saw a flicker of boredom cross the Old Judge's face. The Young Judge, it was clear, was about to make a long-winded speech which the older man had probably heard hundreds of times before.

"Our great ancestor, Kremlin, survived only by a miracle the devastating nuclear war which destroyed cities and countries all over our planet in the year 2102." The Young Judge paused, presumably to allow this information to sink in. He went on, "The cause of that nuclear war was greed, competition, rivalry and lack of orderliness. The civilisations of that world deserved to be destroyed, for they allowed crime and all manner of idleness to flourish.

"Kremlin and the members of his computer team who survived with him resolved to build a new society, one where law and order was maintained, and all were obedient to their rulers, no one was lazy or refused to work. This is the society of Pax City, which you have sought to disturb by your persistent laziness and sloppy work," the Young Judge accused Dierdre, "and you by your rebelliousness," he said turning to Miranda. The Young Judge paused again, glaring furiously at the girls. Miranda felt Dierdre start to tremble again. To comfort her, Miranda drew the child closer. As she did so, Miranda was aware that the Old Judge seemed to be watching her, but when she turned to meet his gaze, he quickly looked away.

The Young Judge had drawn himself up to his full height and looked imposingly across the judgement hall. "We cannot afford to have lazy layabouts and rebels disturbing the peace and order of Pax City," he said ponderously. "My decision is that you should both be executed."

Miranda gasped fearfully, and Dierdre began to cry in terror, burying her face in Miranda's shoulder. There was only one chance now to avert this frightful fate. If the Old Judge did not agree with the Young Judge's decision, he might be able to make him change his mind. If not, then judgement would be given by the computer.

The Old Judge seemed to be pondering his words before he spoke. Miranda waited, cold with trepidation.

"I think your decision is wise and appropriate," he told the Young Judge, who looked smug and satisfied. The smugness faded a little as the Old Judge went on, "But I have been consulting a few statistics during the course of the trial of these two offenders." The Old Judge had a sheaf of papers with him, which he handed across the table to his colleague. The Young Judge frowned as he leafed through them.

"The older one is fifteen," the Old Judge continued, nodding towards Miranda. "The other is eleven. Now, during the years when they were born, there were fewer worker-births in Pax City than ever before. They were the years after the robot rebellion, you remember, and there was much unrest."

Miranda gave a quiet gasp of surprise. She had never heard

"My decision is that you should both be executed."

of the robot rebellion and could not imagine anything so outlandish. The idea of the robots thinking for themselves and getting together to defy the all-powerful rulers of Pax City was quite impossible. Yet, from what the Old Judge had said, it seemed it had indeed taken place. The Young Judge looked impatient. "What's the point of all this?" he asked suspiciously.

The Old Judge gave a sigh. "Well, it's just that we can't afford to get rid of the workers we do have when there aren't enough of them as it is—except for a very serious offence, of course!"

"But is not the peace and orderliness of Pax City more important than these two useless wretched girls?" The Young Judge had leapt to his feet in a passion now.

"Of course it is," the Old Judge assured him smoothly. "But there are other ways of ensuring that these two do not repeat their error and commit disobedience a second time!"

"Oh, not exile outside the city again!" The Young Judge snorted with resentment. Obviously, the two Judges had had this difference of opinion before. "Really, I don't know why you bother. The chances of surviving in the Deadlands outside Pax City are only about one hundred to one. Most offenders we have sent there have never returned. There's nothing but dust and desert and desolation—everyone knows that!"

Miranda and Dierdre exchanged fearful glances. From the sound of it, the Old Judge's decision seemed much worse than the decision of the Young Judge.

"Well, let us compromise then," the Old Judge was saying. "Let us exile them outside the city for three days. If they do not come back—well, it will be much as the same as executing them, as you have decided. If they do come back, do you not think that, having seen the terrible desert outside, these girls will be glad that they live in Pax City, and will make sure they obey our laws in future? And," the Old Judge concluded, "they will tell others of what they have seen, and deter them from wrong doing!"

The Young Judge knew when he had been out-argued, but he did not like it. Frowning and furious, he reluctantly agreed.

As the guardian robots marched them through Pax City towards the outer gate, Miranda half-hoped that the people who thronged the streets would come to their rescue. After all, there were dozens of them and only two guardians; but it was a futile hope. As soon as people spotted Miranda and Dierdre in the firm grip of the robots, they realised what was going on and turned their backs or slipped away down side streets to avoid getting involved. They were afraid, and fear made them selfish.

They reached the gate and once the correct signals had been exchanged with the sentry robots, the gates were swung open. Slowly, the desolate vista outside Pax City was revealed. It was awful, nothing but a flat, featureless plain that stretched to the horizon in all directions. The two girls were pushed through the gates without ceremony, and as the gates slammed shut behind them, there was a strange and sudden silence as all sound from inside Pax City was abruptly cut off. Dierdre was clinging frantically to Miranda's arm, staring about her absolutely horrified, and no wonder. The blackened, blasted Deadlands were just as horrifying as they had always been told, all the more so because neither Miranda nor Dierdre had ever been outside Pax City.

Miranda felt eyes watching her. She looked up at the huge dome encircling Pax City and saw an open porthole just about where she and Dierdre were standing. The lights on the robots' face-dials winked out of the darkness behind it. They were waiting to see what the two girls would do. Miranda knew, without a doubt, that what they had to do was start walking. The two Judges had not put them outside the city just to loiter around until it was time for them to be let in again.

"Come on, Dierdre!" Miranda pulled the child's hand.

"But where are we going? Where can we go?" Dierdre cried plaintively.

"Anywhere, somewhere… I don't know!" Miranda felt horribly afraid as she scanned the flat blackness of the landscape before her, but there was nothing else she could say.

They started walking, the black ground crunching beneath their feet with each step. Grit kept getting caught inside their sandals, and every few minutes they had to halt and shake it out. Before long, Miranda's head began to ache in the intense heat and dryness that seemed to be burning down from the huge fiery orb high above their heads.

"What is it?" Dierdre wanted to know. She gazed up at it, but at once closed her eyes as they began to hurt in its brilliant rays. Miranda shielded her eyes with her hand and took a quick look. It was like gazing into a dazzling blaze of fire. There was nothing like this in Pax City. The light that shone through the high dome there was much less strong and the sky above it was not the same bright blue as it was out here in the Deadlands.

Suddenly, Dierdre knelt down and stared closely at something in the ground. "Look!" she said excitedly. Miranda followed Dierdre's pointing finger and saw a tiny patch of green poking up out of the black rubble.

"There's another one—and another one... Look, over there!" Dierdre exclaimed.

They were like minute jewels sparkling on a deep black cloth. Miranda picked one up and felt a tug before it came away in her hand. It was a leaf, the tiniest leaf she had ever seen, infinitely smaller than the huge leaves on the plants and trees in Pax City's artificial gardens. It felt velvety and moist between her fingers.

Miranda felt a stir of excitement and hope as she realised what this could mean. "There must be water here," she breathed hardly daring to believe it. Perhaps the Deadlands were not so dead as they had at first appeared. Dierdre, enthralled by her discovery, had gone a little way ahead searching for more green leaves. Now, she came running back to Miranda, panting in the heat, but very excited.

"There's a sort of pathway of leaves over there!" she cried. "They get thicker and thicker! Shall we follow them?"

Of course they would follow them. Dierdre's green pathway meant there must be a stream running beneath the desert. Otherwise, the leaves would never have been able to grow.

They proceeded very slowly, partly because of the heat, partly

She must face up to that challenge and survive

because Miranda wanted to make sure they followed the main pathway of green, and did not get side-tracked by scattered off-shoots that led nowhere.

Now Miranda was beginning to understand why people sent out into the Deadlands as a punishment hardly ever came back. Even if they found enough green leaves to eat, they could die from lack of water, or from utter despair at the desolation of their surroundings. Miranda steeled herself against the despair. This was a challenge, these three days out in the Deadlands. She must face up to that challenge and survive. Then she could return to Pax City and give the people there some hope that life was returning to the Deadlands. It was only tiny green leaves today, but it could be trees, and birds and animals tomorrow and perhaps, one day, people could live out here and escape the terrible tyranny of life in the city. Miranda thought of the Old Judge. It had been his idea to send them out into the Deadlands, but the lesson Miranda was learning there was not the one he had had in mind.

Miranda's thoughts were quickly brought back to their present situation as she realised how parched and dry her throat was. From the way Dierdre kept rubbing her neck and trying to swallow, she was obviously suffering the same. Despite the heat and her aching head, Miranda quickened her pace. Dierdre had to scramble to keep up with her.

The green pathway kept meandering this way and that, sometimes doubling back on itself, sometimes going straight for a while, then bending sharply to one side, but Miranda saw with relief that it was, at least, continuous. They had been following it for about an hour and the dome of Pax City, like a vast bubble planted in the desert, had long ago disappeared over the horizon, when Miranda suddenly saw a shimmer a long way in front of them. It seemed to dance just above the surface of the ground, and every now and then sparkled with shafts of light.

"Water—it must be water!" Miranda thought. She began to run, with Dierdre following behind until at last they were able to make out a tall tree crowned with large leaf-shaped fronds and the outline of what looked like a thick forest of reeds. A few minutes later, Miranda and Dierdre stood by the edge of the pool gazing amazed at its shining surface, which kept bubbling up as the underground steam pumped water into it.

It was like finding paradise. The coolness of the water came up at them, refreshing their hot skins. The reeds, a beautiful delicate green, clustered on the other side of the pool nodding in what seemed to Miranda's surprised eyes to be a gentle breeze. Behind them and in front of them and smothering the base of the tall tree was a tangle of deep green plants with little silver berries dotted among them like stars twinkling in the night sky.

Dierdre turned to Miranda in great excitement. "Can we eat them, do you think?" she asked, and without waiting for an answer went racing round the edge of the pool and started gathering up the berries in her skirt. Then she sat herself down and popped one in her mouth.

"Oh, Miranda, they're deeeee-eeelicious!" Dierdre cried. "They taste like... well, all sweet and cool!" They both ate. The berries reminded Miranda of the soft, white fruits that grew in the gardens of Pax City, only these were better: they tasted of fresh air and warmth somehow, because they were growing out here, wild and free.

When Dierdre had eaten as much as she could, she decided she was going to taste the pleasures of the pool. Miranda smiled, happy for the child, as she kicked off her sandals and jumped straight into the pool with a tremendous splash.

"This is marvellous, Miranda! Do come in, do!" Miranda realised it was the very first time she had ever seen Dierdre smile or enjoy herself. Dierdre was having a wonderful time, splashing about in the water, and from time to time diving down below the surface and making a game of popping up unexpectedly in different places in the pool.

Every time she did so, Miranda waved and smiled to her, hoping that Dierdre was far enough away not to detect from her expression that there were some worried thoughts going through her mind. Why had no one ever returned to Pax City to tell of this wonderful place? It was possible to live here for the few days the punishment of exile into the Deadlands lasted. In fact, it was not like punishment at all, but a wonderful experience of freedom and luxury compared to the drabness of life in the city. Yet only a handful of exiles had come back from the Deadlands, and what is more, none Miranda knew had said anything about the cool, shady pool. Why? It was not difficult to find. Others must have spotted the pathway of little green leaves that led here. If Dierdre had detected it, and she was not exactly clever, then anyone could. It was a puzzle and one which Miranda, try as she might, could not explain.

After a while, she gave up and went to the pool side, where she splashed several handfuls of water in her face. At once, the problem that had taxed her was forgotten. Dierdre was right— this was marvellous, absolutely marvellous! Miranda quickly took off her sandals and stepped into the water, letting it rise higher and higher, like soft satin cooling her all over.

Then suddenly, unexpectedly, Miranda heard something. It was only a small noise, but it came at her quite clearly across the dead silence of the surrounding land. Miranda stiffened, alert and watchful.

"What's the matter, Miranda?" Dierdre had turned serious all of a sudden as she detected Miranda's sudden change of mood.

It was a whirring sound, steady and low-pitched, and it was coming nearer and nearer. Miranda looked quickly about her, but could see nothing, yet the sound was still there.

Miranda began wading towards Dierdre. "Get in among those reeds!" she told her urgently.

"But what is it Miranda? Please tell me!" The plaintive wailing was back in Dierdre's voice. Miranda did not reply. She just kept surveying the black landscape all round the pool. Then she saw it: a small, streamlined hovercar, skimming across the ground towards the pool in a whirl of black dust. At once, Miranda dived towards Dierdre, who had not moved, and pushed her in among the reeds. Miranda followed and indicated to Dierdre to duck down, and keep absolutely quiet.

Miranda stiffened, alert and watchful

The hovercar whirred up to the edge of the pool and the engine stopped and it subsided on to the ground. There was a sharp click and one side of the hovercar lifted up. Miranda clamped her hand over her mouth to stop herself gasping as she recognised the figure which emerged.

"A robot! It's a robot!" she hissed to Dierdre.

"You mean a guardian robot? They've come for us already..." Dierdre seemed to be on the edge of tears.

Miranda peered fearfully between the reeds at the silvery figure standing by the edge of the pool. It was not a guardian robot, nor any robot she had seen in Pax City. Their face-dials were square and full of lights. This one had a round face and what seemed like eyes, a nose and a mouth.

"Come with me please! Do not be afraid!" The metallic voice came across to Miranda and Dierdre. They shrank back into the reeds, praying that they might remain unseen.

Miranda realised at once that it was no use hoping. The round-faced robot was staring straight at them.

"Come with me please! Do not be afraid!" it said again.

"It must have some sort of guidance system," Miranda whispered to Dierdre. "How else could it have known we were here?" She stood up in the reeds looking, but not feeling, as bold as she could. "What do you want? What are you doing here?" she said, carefully steadying her voice.

The robot did not reply immediately. It looked down for a moment, as if it was thinking, and then said, "Come with me please! Do not be afraid!"

"Why does it keep saying that?" Dierdre wanted to know.

"I don't think it's programmed to say anything else," Miranda told her.

Quickly, Miranda thought over this sudden, surprising situation. If they went with the robot as it asked, what could they lose? They could not stay here by the pool for ever, marvellous though it was, and the only other alternative was to wait until it was time to go back into Pax City. The thought of returning there chilled Miranda through and through. If there was the slightest chance of avoiding it, by accompanying this robot or doing anything else, she was all for it.

Miranda turned to Dierdre. "We're going to do as it says," she told her firmly. Dierdre opened her mouth to protest but before she could say anything Miranda went on, "I've got a funny feeling it's all right." She had, too. Where this confidence came from, Miranda could not tell. Perhaps there was something in the robot's manner that made her feel it represented no danger. The feeling was confirmed when Miranda and Dierdre waded to the side of the pool and the robot bent down to help them out. Its grip was firm, but gentle, not like the clamping grip of the robots in Pax City.

They followed the robot to the hovercar, where it opened the door and indicated that they should get in. Then it stood back as they climbed inside, to be greeted by a cool breeze of air. It was very pleasant, and the seats in which they settled themselves were extremely comfortable. The robot bent over and started fussing with the seat adjustment button. The seats leaned slowly backwards and Miranda and Dierdre found themselves half-lying on what felt very much like a cushion of air. Miranda had never experienced such marvellous luxury.

"Thank you!" she said to the robot.

The robot inclined its head and then, suddenly its mouth, which had looked like a straight slit, flicked up at the corners.

"What's it doing?" Dierdre whispered curiously.

"I think it's smiling," said Miranda.

The journey took only a few minutes of skimming along across the Deadlands. As it drove the hovercar, the robot looked round once or twice to make sure its passengers were all right. Or at least, that was how it appeared to Miranda. This robot was quite definitely not from Pax City. Of that much, Miranda was now certain. The city robots were stupid things, unable to do very much except by direct command. This robot was skilful enough to drive a hovercar, and it was almost a person, Miranda felt. By the time the journey ended, Miranda discovered she was even growing quite fond of it.

At last, the hovercar came to rest outside a low, flattish dome. For one horrible moment, Miranda thought it was Pax City, but then she realised that it was much smaller. There was another difference, too. From the outside, the dome of the city had looked a dull grey. This one seemed to glow a curious green.

When Miranda and Dierdre were ushered inside, they discovered why. They were in a beautiful forest, or what looked like one. All round them were trees with branches smothered in cool green leaves. Some had circlets of tiny pink and white blossoms growing among them. Lower down, there was a continuous froth of bushes, like great balls of green. On some of them, the leaves were pointed like spearheads, on others, they were like long fronds. Most wonderful of all, and most strange to the astounded gaze of Miranda and Dierdre was the fringe of brilliantly coloured plants, standing up on stalks, a marvellous mass of blues, reds, purples and yellows. A gorgeous scent seemed to emanate from them, making the air inside the dome sweet and a bit heady.

"What are they?" Miranda gasped. She turned to the robot who had driven them to this amazing place, but then remembered that his programming did not include the answer to that, or any other question. The robot just smiled and looked over Miranda's shoulder to where a man was approaching along a path carved out between the trees. Or was it a man? At first sight, it looked like one, but then, as it came closer, Miranda noticed a metallic tinge which told her that this was another robot. All the same, his form was rounded, his face full of expression, and he moved with an easy gait, just as a man would have done. The biggest surprise of all was that he spoke like a man, not in the tinny monotone of a robot.

"Thank you, Klagon," he said to the smiler-robot, "You may go now." Klagon gave a stiff bow in reply, and walked away.

Miranda's eyebrows had shot up with surprise at hearing a robot being addressed by a name. In Pax City, they were known only by numbers. The robot seemed to read her thoughts.

"We all have names here," he explained to Miranda. "Mine is

Or was it a man? At first sight, it looked like one

Robert. How do you do?" and he extended his silvery hand.

"How do I do what?" said Miranda, completely flummoxed.

Robert laughed with a tinny sort of echo. So he was a robot, Miranda thought. "No, you do not understand," he said. "'How do you do' is what our master has taught us to say when we meet people for the first time!"

"Oh, I see!" Miranda replied, not really seeing what he meant at all.

"Ugh, they taste horrible!" It was Dierdre, standing near the brightly coloured plants with her face all screwed up. There was a half-eaten plant in her hand. Miranda was horrified and rushed over to her.

"Dierdre, you naughty girl! Who told you you could touch those plants?" she said crossly.

Robert took the mangled plant from Dierdre's hand and for a moment Miranda thought he was going to be angry with her, but he simply looked sorrowful.

"Oh dear," he said. "That is a pity. Now this flower will die— and it was so beautiful."

"Flower? What is a flower?" said Dierdre, mystified.

"All these are flowers," Robert explained, indicating the fringe of brightly coloured plants. "We grow them for their beauty, so that we will have something lovely to look at. They are not meant to be eaten." Robert suddenly looked abashed. "Oh, but it is my fault," he went on. "I should have warned you. My master told me that in Pax City nothing is grown except to be used in some way, or eaten as food. You have never seen flowers before, have you?"

"No, we haven't ... and we have never seen a place like this before, either!" Miranda's voice was edged with alarm as she spoke. There was too much that was strange and curious here. Her suspicions were aroused. "Where are we? What is this place? And who is your master?" she wanted to know.

"I will take you to him," Robert replied, quite unruffled by Miranda's outburst. "He is waiting for you."

The room was dark, or rather the light in it was soft and restful. Robert showed the two girls in and then quietly closed the door behind them. Dierdre edged towards Miranda and clutched at her hand.

"Miranda, I'm frightened!" she whispered. "I don't like this place ... it's creepy!"

"There is no need to be afraid. There is nothing to fear here!" The voice was kind and gentle, and it seemed to come from the deep shadow across the room. Peering at it, Miranda could just make out a tall figure, who seemed to be seated in a chair.

Miranda gulped with trepidation, and Dierdre pressed herself close to her as the figure rose to its feet and walked slowly across the room. As the man passed through a soft patch of light beaming in towards the centre of the room from the walls, Miranda recognised him.

"Oh, no! Not you!" she whispered in horrified tones.

"Why not me?" said the Old Judge, coming up to them. Miranda and Dierdre cringed back instinctively, so astounded at seeing the man who had sent them out into the terrible Deadlands that they could only goggle at him, open mouthed.

"Why not me?" the Old Judge repeated. "Really, Miranda, I thought you were intelligent enough to guess what I have been doing!"

Before Miranda could bring herself to reply, the Old Judge gave a sympathetic smile. "Well, perhaps it was too much to ask," he said. "Life in Pax City does not exactly encourage anyone to think for themselves, does it? Still, you will never see that terrible place again, either of you. I can promise you that!"

Miranda found her voice at last, and all her questions came in a rush.

"What do you mean? Why have you brought us here? Is it to give us some special punishment?" Dierdre gave a shriek of fright when she heard that and began to cry. Miranda put protective arms around her, and now that she had got over her first shock at seeing the Old Judge here, she felt herself becoming impatient.

The Old Judge looked rueful. "I think I had better explain

things before you get any more wrong ideas, either of you!" he told the two girls. "But first, let me show you something."

The Old Judge went over to the other side of the room and put his hand on a panel in the wall. At once, the panel opened out, revealing a picture. A light glowed around it, and Miranda saw that it was the picture of a lovely woman of about thirty.

"She's beautiful!" Miranda murmured, as she gazed at the picture. Miranda traced her gaze over the lovely face, the warm, friendly eyes and rounded lips that curved in the sweetest of smiles, all of it framed in fair hair that tumbled down to the woman's shoulders like a golden waterfall.

"This is my wife." There was a break in the Old Judge's voice as he spoke, as if he was suddenly overcome by sadness. He sighed deeply. "Or at least, this was how she looked when I last saw her seventeen years ago, seventeen long years..." The Old Judge's words seemed to trail off and Miranda fancied she saw tears glistening in his eyes as he looked at the picture.

"Is she ... is she dead, then?" Miranda whispered.

The Old Judge shook his head. "No, she is alive, but very, very far away!"

The Judge sighed again, and in spite of herself, Miranda was beginning to feel sorry for him.

"But what happened? Why..." Miranda began to ask.

"Why have I shown you her picture?" the Old Judge finished her words for her. "Because you will see her very soon," he explained.

"What?" Miranda gasped in amazement, then realising her outburst was rather rude, she said more quietly, "But how will we see her?"

"It is a long story," the Old Judge replied, "but I will try to make it as brief as possible. You do not have very much time, Miranda. You will have to leave very soon."

Miranda stopped herself asking what he meant by that, or where she and Dierdre were going. She was, by now, far too curious and intrigued to know the Old Judge's story. So was Dierdre, if her wide, surprised eyes were anything to go by.

"Well, as you know, Pax City was created long ago by Kremlin and his team of computer experts," the Judge began. "They had not only survived the holocaust of the nuclear war, they had lived through the time of tension and anger and rivalry that led up to it. So they decided to build a better, more disciplined society, one where people would be more responsible and would not let their arguments drive them to war and violence. It was a wonderful idea, but there was a terrible weakness in it..."

"What was that?" asked Miranda.

"In a society like Pax City," the Old Judge explained. "It was very easy for some harsh, cruel dictator to go too far and exploit for his own evil ends the discipline and obedience to the law which Kremlin tried to create. That is what happened when Nezi, Kremlin's great-great-grandson became the ruler of Pax City twenty years ago. He turned the city into a sort of slave society where people were punished for not obeying the law, instead of being encouraged to keep it. In Pax City, everyone was supposed to work hard and contribute to the good of the whole community; but when Nezi made everyone work hard, it was for his own selfish reasons—so that he and his officials could live in comfort and luxury.

"So that no one would be able to take away his power, Nezi invented the mindsearcher. That way, he would know what everyone was thinking. He also set his scientists to work building the guardian robots to keep the people in order."

"But what has this to do with your wife?" Miranda asked.

"She was one of Nezi's scientists," said the Judge, the sadness coming back into his voice, "but she was like you, Miranda—a rebel. She knew Nezi was evil and wicked, and that somehow he had to be destroyed so that Pax City could once more be as Kremlin envisaged it: the city of peace and co-operation. She secretly programmed the robots so that they would not be as cruel and heartless as Nezi wanted. She arranged their circuits so that they would not go beyond a certain point when it came to punishing people who broke the law. In other words, she gave the robots feelings and sympathy. She wanted them to know

216

when to take pity on people who were being made to suffer by Nezi and his officials."

The Judge paused and wiped his eyes with the back of his hand. He seemed very upset now that he was speaking of his wife, but he managed to continue. "Unfortunately, she did her work too well. Something went wrong, and the robots became so sympathetic towards the people and came to hate Nezi so much that they rebelled."

The Judge looked grim, as he recalled all the terrible events that had occurred. "Many people were killed and Pax City was almost destroyed before the rebellion was brought under control. A new, more obedient breed of robots was constructed and all the old ones were destroyed, except for a few my wife and I managed to save and bring here."

"Is Robert one of them—and Klagon?" Miranda asked, suddenly realising why the robots had been so kind.

"Yes," the Old Judge told her. "But my wife altered their circuits again to make them a bit calmer and less hot-tempered. Then, one day, she went to the city to see if there were any more robots she could rescue. She never came back!" The Old Judge could speak the last few words only with difficulty.

"What happened?" Miranda asked gently.

"Nezi had discovered what she had been doing. He ordered her to be executed. I pleaded for her, and even offered to die in her place, and at last Nezi agreed that she should be exiled for ever to a far distant planet." The Old Judge bowed his head in distress at the frightful memories of that time, and Miranda felt impelled to go up to him, and put a comforting hand on his arm.

"You are very much like her, Miranda," he said brokenly. "Kind, compassionate, and not afraid to speak out or act against what you think is wrong … That was why you defended little Dierdre here from the Work Officer."

Miranda looked puzzled. "Didn't you realise why you did it?" the Old Judge asked in surprise.

"Well, no. I thought I was simply being disobedient…" Miranda shook her head, unable to work out her reasons. "I didn't

Deirdre crept up to where the Old Judge sat

really know why I did it. I only knew ... thought ... that the Work Officer was being cruel and unjust..."

The Judge nodded sadly. "Yes, the rulers of Pax City would like you to believe that compassion, kindness and pity are wrong. They just want you to work and obey and never think for yourselves at all! They want you to be mindless slaves. It is easier for them to keep their power that way." For a moment, the Old Judge's voice had an angry tinge to it, but then he seemed to lapse once more into his mood of sadness.

Dierdre had crept up to where the Old Judge sat, completely free now of her former fear of him. Both she and Miranda had heard quite enough now to know that the Old Judge was their friend and protector, and that their previous opinion of him had been quite wrong. Dierdre knelt down by the Old Judge's feet and he put out a hand and lifted her chin up a little, regarding her with a soft, kind expression.

"Where my wife is now, children like you are treated kindly," he said softly. "You are not very clever or very skilful, are you Dierdre? Well, where my wife is, you will be helped to become a little better at your work."

"But where is she? Where is your wife?" Miranda was eager to know.

In reply, the Judge got to his feet and led them to another side of the room where the roof panels stood half open. Miranda realised with a start that it was now quite dark outside. Directly underneath the open panels, there stood a large telescope, pointing up at the sky. The Old Judge helped Miranda to climb the steps and settle herself in the seat. Then he turned the huge cylinders at the base of the telescope, looked through it and told Miranda, "That's where she is! Look for yourself!"

Miranda looked through the eyepiece. The telescope was trained on a large, shining orb, magnifying it many times so that Miranda was able to see triangular patches on it. There was also a swirl of what looked like clouds hovering over it. A little way above the orb was a much smaller one which seemed to be moving round it. As Miranda watched, the small orb disappeared behind the big one, then reappeared again as it progressed in its orbit.

"What is it?" Miranda asked the Judge. "It looks like ... like another world far, far away!"

"It is far away," said the Judge. "It is called Earth and that tiny orb going round it is called Moon. It is very beautiful there—full of trees, and flowers and covered in a soft green plant called grass. Or at least the land is... my wife has told me that there are huge, vast oceans full of water there, covering most of the planet..."

Miranda was amazed. "Your wife told you? But how?"

The Judge smiled and Miranda was very pleased to see it. "Ah, well you see, Miranda, my wife was not a scientist for nothing. As soon as the prison ship landed on Earth, she began to construct a radio system for getting in touch with me. She told me what Earth was like and what grew there and how beautiful it was, and so I constructed a garden here, in this dome, so that she and I would at least be able to live in the same surroundings." Miranda looked puzzled, not quite understanding this. "You passed through it on your way to this room..." he said. "Was it not very beautiful?"

"You mean Earth is like that?" Miranda gasped. "All green, and full of colour and sweet smelling air? It must be wonderful!" Then, a sudden thought occurred to her. "But if it is so wonderful, and your wife is there, why have you not gone to join her?"

"I will, one day," the Old Judge told her. "But not until my work is finished here."

"Your work?"

"You have still not guessed, have you Miranda?" the Old Judge smiled. "Do you not remember that it was I who persuaded the Young Judge to agree to send you out of Pax City into the Deadlands for three days? You and little Dierdre here are only the latest among hundreds who have been punished that way for breaking the law or for showing disobedience or for protesting against the Work Officer... and all at my suggestion! I have gained quite a reputation in Pax City for being harsh and cruel because of it," the Judge went on ruefully. "It is understandable. Most offenders have never come back from the Deadlands, have they? Some have died out there, it is true, out of despair or terror at finding themselves in that ghastly place, but many others did not die..."

"But where did they go?" Miranda was still puzzled.

"They were brought here," was the reply. "Like you, they found the green trail that led to the pool... that was the test. I created that pool for the purpose. You see, those who found it showed they had enterprise and the will to live, and a spirit strong enough not to be broken by the cruelty and oppression of Pax City. That was the sort of spirit they would need when they reached the planet Earth."

"What do you mean?"

The Judge could not answer Miranda's question immediately. Dierdre, fascinated by all she had heard, demanded to be allowed to see the beautiful planet, and it was several minutes before she was satisfied, and allowed the Old Judge to lift her down from the telescope seat.

Miranda stood by, impatiently at first, but then she began to work out for herself what the Judge had meant. She remembered how kind he had been when she had come into the judgement hall with Dierdre, and he had warned the Young Judge against being needlessly cruel. Now, Miranda realised she had been right when she felt he was trying to help her, that he was not in any way as stern and unsympathetic as she had, at first, imagined. Now, there was this revelation about his wife, and what had happened to her. There could be only one ending to it, and at last it dawned on Miranda what it was.

"You have been sending all those people to Earth, to your wife, haven't you?" she told the Old Judge. "That's where you're going to send Dierdre and me..."

The Old Judge put his arms about both of them in an affectionate gesture.

"Yes," he said quietly. "There is a transporter room here, and they have all been sent to Earth that way. It was too dangerous

A lovely warmth seemed to enclose Miranda

to send them in rocket ships—the Pax City Space Force might have intercepted them and shot them down. I will take you to the transporter room very soon, but first let me tell you this." The Old Judge regarded them both a little gravely, then went on, "You will be able to start a new life on Earth, with my wife to guide and help you, but don't think it will be an easy life. There is much work to be done, and you must learn to co-operate with everyone else, and settle any problems or disputes peacefully and in a disciplined way—just as Kremlin wanted us to do here. So you will need all your spirit, enterprise and determination."

The Old Judge's voice had a final tone about it, and Miranda realised that the time had now come for them to leave. The Old Judge summoned Robert, who came immediately, and together they escorted the two girls further along the pathway in the Earth forest which the Old Judge had created. When they reached the transporter room, the pads on which Miranda and Dierdre had to stand were all ready for them. Robert went over to the large console nearby and programmed it with the co-ordinates for direction Earth. A lovely warmth seemed to enclose Miranda and Dierdre as the transporting process began, and the last thing they remembered seeing before they began their journey across deep space was the Judge's smile, and his arm raised in greeting as he bad them farewell.

The Old Judge stood for a while, staring at the empty places Miranda and Dierdre had occupied, allowing himself to daydream for a moment about his beloved wife and the beautiful planet Earth and the vast chasm of space which lay between them. He was woken from his reverie by Robert's hand, gently laid on his arm.

"It is time to return to the city, master!" Robert reminded him. The Old Judge nodded and moved towards the door of the transporter room. Robert was right. There was no time to be spent daydreaming. The next trial in the judgement hall would begin in only two hours.

"Tell Klagon to get the hovercar," the Old Judge told Robert crisply. "I shall leave immediately!"